LOSTMAN'S RIVER

CYNTHIA DeFELICE

AN AVON CAMELOT BOOK

The author wishes to gratefully acknowledge Mr. Billy L. Cypress, executive director of the Seminole Museum in Hollywood, Florida, for contributing to the story's accuracy, and Captain Robert S. Collins, Jr., of Naples, Florida, for guiding her up Lostman's River.

AVON BOOKS, INC.
1350 Avenue of the Americas
New York, New York 10019

Copyright © 1994 by Cynthia C. DeFelice
Published by arrangement with Macmillan Publishing Company, Inc.
Library of Congress Catalog Card Number: 93-40857
ISBN: 0-380-72396-4
RL: 5.5
www.avonbooks.com

First Avon Camelot Printing: October 1995

CAMELOT TRADEMARK REG U S PAT OFF AND IN OTHER COUNTRIES, MARCA REGISTRADA, HECHO EN U S A

Printed in the U.S.A.

OPM 10 9 8 7 6 5

With love and thanks to
Beverly Reingold,
Frank Hodge,
and all the Hodge-Podgers

bad luck, even though I didn't set as much store in such things as some folks did.

"Good day," the man called. "Come help a fellow make a proper landing, won't you?"

I could see that he was going to make a mess of coming ashore, headed straight into land as he was. I ran to the edge of the water and grabbed the front of the canoe before it could run aground. It took all my strength to stop the forward motion. Quickly, with my right hand, I grabbed the gunwale and pulled the rear of the canoe around until the boat sat sideways to the shoreline. The man stepped out, nearly tipping the canoe over, but he appeared not to notice. I pulled it up, wondering at the man's carelessness, leaving a boat where it would be carried off by the river in no time flat.

The man, meanwhile, was smoothing his hair, straightening his hat, and—I could hardly believe my eyes— tightening a tie he wore at the collar of his white, stiff-looking shirt. Now that he was out of the canoe and standing before me, I could see that he was a small man, no taller than I was, and very neat and tidy-looking. He held out his hand to me and said, "Hugo M. Strawbridge, naturalist and collector." He reached into his shirt pocket and produced a small piece of paper, which he handed to me, saying, "My card."

I examined the paper, figuring that was what he meant for me to do. It said: *Hugo M. Strawbridge, Naturalist and Collector. Member of the Royal Academy of Sciences of Paris, Fellow of the Royal Societies of London and Edinburgh, the*

Linnaean and Zoological Societies of London, and the Natural Historical Society of Paris, procurer for the Smithsonian Institution and the American Museum of Natural History.

I'd never seen so many big words all strung together like that. Mama had taught me to read, of course, from her old Bible. There were some big words in the Bible, *Deuteronomy* and *Leviticus* and such, but some of the words on that card appeared to me to be in a foreign language, like Latin or French, maybe. I stood staring at the man, probably looking like some kind of dim-witted fool, until I realized that handing me that card had been his way of introducing himself.

"Tyler MacCauley," I said, shaking his hand quickly. He lifted an eyebrow, as if waiting for me to say something else, but I didn't have a "card" or big words to add after my name.

Mama came out of the house, the line between her eyes deep with worry. She looked at me, a question in her eyes. "Ty?"

Before I could say anything, the little man launched into his introduction all over again. Mama nodded faintly when he had finished, and I knew she was as puzzled as I was. She, too, shook Mr. Strawbridge's hand. Then she said in a low voice, "What is it you want here, Mr. Strawbridge?"

"Mr. Strawbridge has the sacred duty of procuring specimens of nature's bounty and beauty, both for the edification of the populace and the furthering of scientific knowledge. To this end, Mr. Strawbridge seeks the aid and assistance of an able-bodied companion, someone who is familiar with the local flora and fauna, someone with the knowledge and ability to guide Mr. Strawbridge on this expedition in the hallowed name of science."

At first I thought maybe I'd gotten the introduction part wrong, the way he was talking about Mr. Strawbridge as if he were somebody who wasn't even here. I'd never met a man who talked about himself using his own name like that, but that's who he was speaking of, all right, because next he turned to me and said, "Might you be such a companion, and might you be willing to be my partner in this undertaking?"

I swallowed and started to answer, but before I could say anything the little man added, "I'll pay you the sum of three dollars a day, if you prove to be worth it."

Three dollars a day. The words seemed to hang in the warm, damp air, echoing over and over. Three dollars a day. More than Pa and I made working together, cutting buttonwood. A lot more.

I wasn't exactly sure what it was he was asking me to do, so I didn't know what to say. I looked at Mama for help, and was astonished to see that she was smiling sweetly at Mr. Strawbridge and saying, "Goodness gracious, Mr. Strawbridge, you'll think our good manners have forsaken us altogether, making you stand out here in this heat after your long trip upriver. We don't get much company, you see, but that's no excuse for rudeness, none at all. Why don't you come on in the house now. I'll fix you a nice glass of lemonade, and you can tell us all about your journey."

I watched as Mama took Mr. Strawbridge's arm and

led him into the house, talking all the time. Her voice, usually low and flat and quiet, sounded different, higher and full of music. Her laugh, like the cry of some strange bird, drifted back to me from the doorway as she called, "Tyler, go tell your father we have company for supper!"

I ran to where Pa was still at work making charcoal. "Pa," I blurted, "better come. Mama says to tell you we have company for supper."

Pa's eyes widened with surprise. His face was blackened from tending the smoking pile of wood, and the blue and the whites of his eyes stood out bright and sharp.

"Company?" he repeated. "What kind of company? Don't tell me that scoundrel Bean Thompson is here to scrounge some more of your mama's cooking."

Pa called Bean a scoundrel, but I knew he was only joking. Bean lived out on Hog Key, and was the closest thing to a friend Pa had around here. He'd stop by from time to time, usually just about supper hour.

Bean had told me he got his name 'cause of the way he was so tall and skinny, just like a string bean. But for a skinny man, he sure could eat. Mama would keep offering, and Bean would keep saying, "Why, sure, ma'am, as long as you're asking, I'd dearly love just one more plateful." And Mama would roll her eyes at Pa, and Carrie and I would kick each other under the table and try hard not to laugh.

When Bean was finally full up, he and Pa would play

cards, and sometimes they let me play, too. Bean said if he didn't know better he'd think I was a regular riverboat gambler, the way I won so many games.

"Leave me my shorts, Ty," he'd joke. "It's plain bad manners to send a guest home stark naked."

Mama pretended she didn't like it when Bean showed up, but I knew she loved him as much as Carrie and I did, and Pa laughed more when Bean was around than any other time. I wished I could tell Pa it was Bean who was here for supper, but it wasn't.

"No, Pa," I answered. "It's somebody else. Mr. Something-or-other Strawbridge. From London or New York or Paris, I don't know. Better come quick."

Pa shook his head as if to say what now?, pretty much the way I had. He banked earth up around the smoking wood so it wouldn't catch fire and turn into a full-out blaze. Then we began to walk to the house together. Pa's jaw was set hard, and I could see a little twitch in the side of his face right near his ear.

"He says I can make three dollars a day working for him, Pa, maybe more if I'm good at it."

"Is that right," Pa said. "Good at what?"

"That's the part I couldn't quite make out," I said. "He uses lots of big words, Pa. You'll see."

As we got near to the house, we could hear Mama speaking to Mr. Strawbridge in her happy new voice. Pa stopped to listen.

"Why, I can hardly imagine a cultured gentleman such as yourself making this awful trip," Mama was saying.

"Did the skeeters—I mean to say, did the *mosquitoes* try to simply carry you away?"

Pa began walking toward the door, and I followed.

"They are indeed fierce, madam, but are they not part of God's creation, just as we ourselves are? Do they not deserve—"

When Pa and I walked in, Mama looked flustered and began the introductions. She tried to tell Pa all the important-sounding words that followed Mr. Strawbridge's name. Finally she just laughed and said, "You go on and tell him yourself, Mr. Strawbridge."

Mr. Strawbridge wasn't shy about bragging, which is what his big talking was beginning to sound like to me. He told Pa the whole business, the same way it was written on the card. Pa just put out his hand and said, "Will MacCauley."

There was quiet while Pa and Mr. Strawbridge looked at each other. Pa was a big man, but standing over Mr. Strawbridge he looked huge.

Mama broke the silence. "Tyler, I was telling Mr. Strawbridge about all the pictures you've sketched, ever since you were a little boy. Maybe after supper you can show them to him."

"Sure," I said, but I felt embarrassed to show Mr. Strawbridge my drawings, and I hoped Mama would forget about it later. I liked to draw, but I didn't have much in the way of paper, just what our supplies from the trading post came wrapped in. I used Mama's good pen and ink when she let me. But the drawings were just pictures of things I saw, mostly birds and fish and animals. I didn't suppose Mr. Strawbridge would think too much of them.

Turning back to our visitor and smiling, Mama said, "And perhaps over supper you'll tell us all about what it's like in London and France these days. We've been away so long, you see."

I smiled. The way she said it, it almost sounded as if we'd been all those places ourselves before we came to Florida.

Before Mr. Strawbridge could answer, Pa said, "Maybe right now you can tell me what it is you want with Tyler here."

Mama looked sharply at Pa, and I knew what she was thinking. Pa's words did sound rude, spoken out so suddenlike, but he was always one for getting down to business.

Mr. Strawbridge seemed glad to look away from Pa and over to me. "I was hoping that your son would join me on a scientific expedition. Our aim would be to observe and to collect specimens of the local flora and fauna in order to—"

Pa interrupted. "Speak plain, Mr. Strawbridge, if you're able."

Mr. Strawbridge seemed to shrink even further under Pa's stern gaze, and I was almost beginning to feel sorry for him. But couldn't he just talk like normal folks?

"I'd like to hire your son, Tyler, here, to"—Mr. Strawbridge spoke slowly, feeling his way, it seemed, through all the words in his head—"go with me, to be my guide, so to speak, to help me compile a record of the species—of the kinds—of creatures that live in this part of the state of Florida. Museums and scientific organizations pay me to do this work, and I, in turn, would like to pay your son for his help." He stopped, but Pa didn't speak. Looking nervously at Mama, Mr. Strawbridge added, "That is, of course, if you can spare the boy's labor and if the idea meets with your approval."

"How much?" asked Pa.

"I beg your pardon?" asked Mr. Strawbridge.

"How much are you willing to pay the boy?"

"I offered three dollars a day, sir, which I think you'll agree is quite generous, and represents more income than he is likely to earn in other pursuits."

"Who sent you?" Pa asked.

Mr. Strawbridge looked startled at the sudden change of subject. "Why, it was the Seminole gentleman who brought me here, a Mr. Jumper, I believe his name was."

"Tommy's father!" I said.

"Communication was difficult, at best. I tried to persuade him to join me in my undertaking, but he didn't seem interested. He brought me here."

"Jumper guided you here, but who sent you?" Pa asked again, and his eyes looked as if they might just see through Mr. Strawbridge's head and read the answer there. "How'd you know to come here to find Tyler?"

"Why, I told Mr. Stranahan at the trading post in Fort Lauderdale what I hoped to accomplish, and he suggested I inquire at Brown's Boat Landing in Big Cypress.

Brown sent me on to Mr. George Storter's store in Everglade. It was Storter who gave me your name and told me you had a boy old enough to be of assistance. He arranged for Mr. Jumper to bring me here."

Pa relaxed some at that. I guessed he was glad to hear nobody from up north had sent Mr. Strawbridge after us, or maybe he was glad Mr. Strawbridge wasn't another one of R. J. Munroe's men.

Pa's manner of questioning seemed to be making Mr. Strawbridge uncomfortable. He tugged at his tie, pulled it down loose, and unbuttoned the top button of his shirt. "If you'll pardon me, madam," he said, looking at Mama.

"Oh, Mr. Strawbridge," said Mama, "we don't stand on ceremony here. Please make yourself comfortable. Although I must admit it's nice to see a man dressed like a gentleman, for a change."

Pa scowled. I looked at his shirt, gray from many washings, damp now and stained with sweat and soot from his charcoal making. I felt Mama had shamed him somehow, without meaning to. But what was Pa supposed to do, make charcoal in a white shirt and tie?

Pa turned to me. "It's up to you, son," he said.

"It is?" I said stupidly. I felt confused, as if there were too many things happening at once. I wanted to talk with Pa, just the two of us, but he had turned to the basin to wash up for supper. Mr. Strawbridge and Mama and Carrie were looking at me, waiting for me to answer. I could see the hope in Mama's eyes.

"Well, sure," I said. "I could help out, I guess."

FIVE

Supper was downright uncomfortable that night. Mama asked Mr. Strawbridge all about what it was like in the big cities like New York and London and Paris. Mr. Strawbridge didn't seem to be able to answer a question with a simple word or two, but went on and on about the "elegance of a bygone age" and the "height of culture and refinement." Mama kept nodding her head and sighing.

Then he began talking about the birds and flowers and plants that grow all around these parts, and how they were all so pretty and special. He was right about that, at least.

The more Mr. Strawbridge spoke, the quieter Pa grew, until Pa's silence was the loudest thing in the room. We all sat, fidgeting in our chairs, until finally Pa said, "Will you be leaving in the morning, Mr. Strawbridge?"

Mama sucked in her breath real loud at Pa asking a guest right out when he was planning to leave. But Pa just looked at Mr. Strawbridge, waiting for an answer.

"Why, yes, certainly," Mr. Strawbridge said, looking flustered. "There's no reason why the boy and I can't leave first thing in the morning. I've been well supplied by Mr. Storter at the trading post, and I believe that we are equipped for an expedition of, oh, perhaps two weeks' duration." He coughed and glanced quickly from Mama to Pa. "There seems no reason, I suppose, to delay our departure," he concluded.

"You'll return the boy in two weeks' time and pay him what he's owed?" Pa asked.

"Yes, of course," said Mr. Strawbridge.

"Well, that's settled then," said Pa. He looked at me and said, "You'll be wanting to turn in early, Tyler."

"Just a minute now, Will," said Mama. There was a tone in her voice that I recognized. When Mama sounded like that, she meant business. "I think Mr. Strawbridge would enjoy a day's rest before he heads out on a two-week journey. Wouldn't you, Mr. Strawbridge?" she asked.

"Well, that's a kind invitation, Mrs. MacCauley," Mr. Strawbridge said, smiling at Mama. "A brief respite from my travels would be welcome indeed." His smile fluttered uncertainly when he turned and saw the look on Pa's face. "But, of course, I have no wish to impose upon your kindness," he added quickly. "Perhaps it would be best if we did leave first thing in the—"

Mama interrupted, "Nonsense, Mr. Strawbridge. I won't hear of it. It's a pleasure for us to have such a cultured gentleman as our guest. I only wish that our rustic circumstances allowed us to offer more in the way of hospitality."

There was an awkward silence. Mr. Strawbridge said

quietly, "Your hospitality is impeccable, madam. I thank you."

Pa stood up without excusing himself and headed for the door. I got up to follow Pa, but Mama said sharply, "Sit down, Tyler. Just because your father has lost his manners is no reason for you to do the same. Now, excuse yourself properly, and you and Carrie clear this table."

Mama and Mr. Strawbridge kept on talking while Carrie and I washed the dishes. I felt funny inside, the way things were happening so fast. Here I was, going away for two whole weeks, and I didn't know how I felt about it at all. It seemed to be making Pa mad somehow, but whether he was mad at me or Mama or Mr. Strawbridge I couldn't quite figure out.

While we worked, Carrie whispered to me, "Why are you going with him, Ty?"

"Mr. Strawbridge says he'll pay me lots of money, that's why," I answered her. "Then I can buy you some candy and a new dress and maybe a doll."

"I don't want another doll," said Carrie. "I want a knife, same as yours." ·

I laughed and reached for the leather sheath I kept hanging from my pants. That knife was the best thing I owned, a present Pa had given me when I'd turned thirteen. It was handy for all kinds of work around the place, but I liked most to use it to carve figures out of wood. I had made a whole set of little animals for Carrie, and I'd started on a surprise for Mama: figures for a crèche at

Christmas. I'd already carved Mary and Joseph and baby Jesus lying in the manger. I planned on making the three wise men, maybe have them riding on camels if I could make them look right. And I'd make the donkey, and all the other animals in the stable. I thought I'd even carve an angel to hang over the whole thing. I couldn't wait to see Mama's face when she saw it. But I didn't think Mama would approve of Carrie having a knife, young as she was.

"We'll have to see about that," I said, reaching over to muss Carrie's hair. Carrie was a pest a lot of the time, but that night, thinking about not seeing her for two whole weeks, I felt sort of kindly toward her.

She looked up at me, a frown on her round, freckly face. "I don't like him, Ty. He talks funny."

"Shhh," I said, laughing. "He'll hear you." I leaned over and whispered in her ear a long string of nonsense words, making my voice sound high like Mr. Strawbridge's and using his Yankee way of talking, and Carrie giggled and giggled.

"Tyler," Mama called. "Mr. Strawbridge says he'd like to see your drawings."

I made a face at Carrie and headed to our room to get the box where I kept my pictures. There was no use in arguing: When Mama set her mind on something, it stayed set. I looked quickly through the drawings, chose four I liked the best, and carried them over to the table where Mr. Strawbridge and Mama were sitting.

"They're not much," I said, handing them to the little man. "Just birds and animals and stuff like that."

Mr. Strawbridge took the pictures and looked them over slowly. Then he looked up at me and said, "These are really very good, Tyler, especially for a young man who has had no formal training. You have a very good eye, and a delicate touch. Tell me, have you ever seen the works of John James Audubon?"

"I've heard of him, sir," I answered. "He's some kind of Yankee bird lover. His name gets the plume hunters all riled up, that's for sure. But I didn't know he drew pictures."

"Oh, my, yes, he's become quite famous for his drawings, especially of birds. Your pictures remind me of some of his early work. You have talent, Tyler, did you know that?"

I could feel myself blushing, but Mama was beaming. "You see what I mean, Mr. Strawbridge?" she exclaimed. "That's a perfect example of what I've been saying. How is Tyler supposed to develop his God-given talent in a place like this?"

"Mama, I can draw here same as anywhere else," I protested.

But Mama didn't want to hear any of that. "You two go on to bed now," she said to Carrie and me. "Ty, tomorrow we'll get your things together for the trip."

I didn't have much to get together, anyway, just another set of trousers and a shirt, and maybe a blanket. Carrie and I went to the room we shared in the corner of the house. I heard Mama showing Mr. Strawbridge where he could settle on some blankets in the front room, apologizing over and over again for what she called our "lack of accommodations." Then she, too, went to bed.

I guessed I was glad Mama hadn't forgotten about showing Mr. Strawbridge my drawings. He'd said they were good, but he'd probably seen lots better. I felt restless, thinking about leaving for two weeks with Mr. Strawbridge and wondering where Pa had gone to and when he was coming back. Finally I heard the door open and close and his footsteps cross to the room where he and Mama slept. Soon I could tell from the rise and fall of their voices that they were arguing. I couldn't hear everything, but I did hear enough to know that it had something to do with Mr. Strawbridge's coming. I hoped that he couldn't hear them, too.

It was a long time before I fell asleep. I lay staring into the darkness, listening to Carrie breathing and Mama and Pa whispering, and wondered why on earth I had agreed to go with the strange little man who was snoring lightly in the front room. Because of the money, that's why, I told myself. I couldn't help wishing I'd had more of a chance to talk the idea over with Pa, but Pa hadn't seemed much in the mood to talk since Mr. Strawbridge arrived.

I wondered if it was too late to change my mind.

In the morning Mama and Mr. Strawbridge were up before I was. I left Carrie still sleeping and went into the front room, where Mama was making biscuits and talking with Mr. Strawbridge. Pa was nowhere to be seen. I said a quick good morning and slipped out the door.

I found Pa out by the stacks of buttonwood we'd cut together. He wasn't working. He was just staring at the piles of wood and the smaller piles of charcoal he'd made so far. I walked over and picked up a chunk of charcoal. Pa was right: It was surprisingly light. But messy. I looked down at my blackened fingers and wiped them on my pants leg.

"Sure you don't need me around here to help out, Pa?" I asked.

He shook his head without looking at me. "The work's not hard, son," he said. Then he looked up and a little smile crossed his face. "It's not your labor I'll miss, it's the company. Charcoal making's a lonely, boring business, I've found."

"I'll stay, Pa," I said eagerly. "I'll tell Mr. Strawbridge to—"

"No," Pa said. "You go with the man."

"But, Pa, I—"

"Have you added up what three dollars a day for two weeks comes to?" he asked.

I tried to figure it quickly in my head. "Twenty-one dollars a week?" I said.

Pa nodded.

"Forty-two dollars all told," I said, not really able to imagine that much money all at once.

Pa nodded again. He pointed at the piles of wood and charcoal in front of him. "You know what we're likely to get for that?" he asked.

I shook my head.

"Nine dollars, maybe twelve if we're lucky."

I looked at the stacks of wood and thought of the weeks Pa and I had spent cutting and hauling in the hot sun till our backs felt as if they were breaking. And we still had to load the charcoal onto the raft and take it to the trading post before we'd get so much as a nickel.

"Your mother wants to buy a sewing machine, Tyler, and cloth for dresses and new shirts and curtains and such, and books for you and Carrie, and other things to make her life here better. I guess she'd like anything that could help her feel like she wasn't here at all, but back in New York. Nine dollars won't do it, not after we've bought the supplies we need just to get by."

He stopped for a minute and looked down at his hands. Then, looking back up at me, he said, "So you go with the man, Ty. I don't like it. I don't like him. But I expect I've made life hard enough for your mama, and I can't see my way to keeping her from having a few nice things."

I didn't know what to say. It seemed as if Pa was deciding whether or not to say something else, so I waited.

"Your mama's got a lot of grit, you know," he said finally. "Not many women would have stood by me the way she has."

I nodded, wanting him to keep talking.

"I say I want your mama to have the money you can earn. But you understand, it isn't really *things* she wants. It's a whole way of life she's missing. A few trinkets from the trading post won't make up for everything she's given up to come here, and everything she figures you and Carrie are missing out on. But I don't know what I can do about that. And until I figure it out, well, a little extra money might ease some of her burden."

"You're not mad about me going, then?" I asked.

Pa looked surprised. "Mad? At you, son? Of course not." He stood up and put his arm around my shoulder. "This will be a chance for you to get out on your own, have some real responsibility. You'll do fine." Then, holding me out at arm's length, he smiled and added, "If you can stand up to two weeks of that man's infernal blabbering, you're a better man than I am."

I grinned at that, and we started back to the house together.

"Pa," I asked, "how come you don't like him? Just on account of how he talks so much?"

Pa didn't answer me right away. When he did, I could barely hear him, and I got the feeling he wasn't really talking to me, but more to himself. "When I heard your mama's voice last night, heard the music in it, and the laughter . . ." He stopped. "Then I walked inside and saw her face. It was . . . glowing."

I nodded, remembering Mama's high spirits the night before. Pa stopped walking and looked off toward the river, but I was pretty sure it wasn't the water and the mangroves he was seeing, but Mama's face. "There was a time," he said softly, "when her face lit up like that when she looked at me."

SIX

Pa announced at breakfast that he'd be spending the day burning down the last few charcoal piles. Mr. Strawbridge asked if he "might be of assistance," but Pa quickly said that there was no need for that. Mr. Strawbridge tried his best to appear disappointed, but I thought it was a look of relief I saw cross his face.

"You're to rest up from your journey," Mama told him.

"Well, in that case," said Mr. Strawbridge, turning to me and Carrie, "perhaps the two of you would be willing to show me around your place here."

Carrie looked at me to see how I'd answer. I shrugged. "Sure," I said.

"There's not much to see, I'm afraid," said Mama. "There's the garden, and the orchard, and after that, mangrove trees. Nothing but mangroves and more mangroves."

"Ahhh, the mangrove," said Mr. Strawbridge. "A very interesting species. Did you know—"

"If you'll excuse me," said Pa, standing up from the table, "I'll be getting to work now."

"Why," said Mama, still talking to Mr. Strawbridge,

49

"sometimes I could swear those mangrove trees are walking. The way those long branches grow down into the water, they look like skinny legs. I feel some days that they're creeping closer and closer and one day they'll just—surround me, choke me—"

Mama stopped when she saw Carrie's face. "Carrie, honey, I'm just talking. You don't have to worry about the mangroves. They won't hurt you."

"I know," said Carrie, but she came over and stood by me as she looked toward the doorway.

"Come," said Mr. Strawbridge, "let us go examine the mangrove up close and perhaps you will see what I find so fascinating about it."

The four of us eased past the big palmetto leaf that Mama had hanging in the doorway to brush the mosquitoes off folks coming into the house. It didn't work too well. It was the rainy season, and that meant skeeters. Lots of 'em.

"I suppose it's time to get out the smudge pots," said Mama with a sigh. I knew she hated to do it. The oily black smoke from the pots curled all around the house, inside and out, covering our skin with a greasy soot, filling our noses with its burning smell and our mouths with its bitter taste.

Mama could stand it for just so long. Every year, about halfway through the summer, she'd say she'd had enough. "I'd rather have mosquitoes than this constant smoke and filth," she'd declare, and she'd put out the smudge pots and scrub the house and make us clean up real good, too. But soon after, weeping with despair over the devilish pestering of the skeeters, she'd light the pots again.

Mr. Strawbridge led us out to the stand of mangroves that bordered the riverbank.

"How many different kinds of mangroves do you think there are here in Florida, Tyler?" he asked.

"A mangrove's a mangrove, I guess," I said.

Mr. Strawbridge shook his head and chuckled. "I'm surprised an observant boy like you hasn't noticed that there are three separate species. At least, three that have been identified so far. Of course, scientists have given them Latin names, but for our purposes they can be called simply the red, black, and white mangroves."

"Those are red," said Carrie, pointing to the nearest tree. I looked at the mounds of dark, shiny green leaves and wondered at first what she was talking about. But then I saw the long, skinny branches Mama had been speaking of earlier. They *were* a reddish color.

"That's right, Carrie," said Mr. Strawbridge, beaming at her. "And what you referred to before as branches, Mrs. MacCauley, are in fact roots, what we call prop roots. But you are correct in thinking that they are reaching out with those roots, walking in a sense, farther and farther all the time, taking over new territory. And now," he went on, "who can say what is the single most peculiar and amazing fact about these trees we see all around us?"

No one answered. What was amazing about mangroves? They were as common as water and sky and skeeters.

"Can you drink salt water?" Mr. Strawbridge asked me.

"Not unless I want to get good and sick," I answered.

"Most plants can't drink it, either," Mr. Strawbridge said. "But the mangrove can. It thrives on salt water."

"The river's not always salty," I said. "Like right now, it's mostly fresh water 'cause of the rainy season. It's during the winter when it's salty from the seawater coming up."

"That's right, Tyler," Mr. Strawbridge said, smiling at me as if I'd said something real smart. "Another amazing feat of the mangrove is its ability to adapt to such changes in its surroundings. Just *how* it is able to do that is what interests scientists. Now, red mangroves live all up and down every coastline here, growing right out into the shallow bays, so it is evident that they can tolerate even the saltiest water.

"But I've noticed that the black mangroves grow back farther, along the water's edge, and the white mangroves back even farther, above the tide line. This has led me to the hypothesis that the black mangrove is less tolerant of salt than the red mangrove, and the white even less so. But to prove that hypothesis scientifically requires evidence."

Mr. Strawbridge stopped and smiled at us expectantly, his eyebrows raised, his cheeks flushed from excitement or the heat, I couldn't tell which. Mama, Carrie, and I all smiled back uncertainly. Was he waiting for us to produce the evidence?

But then he went on talking. "As part of our work, Tyler, you and I will be collecting samples of the roots, leaves, and flowers of all the mangrove types for future microscopic study. And I'd like you to try your hand at drawing the different types, showing the differences in their structures and root systems. I've brought paints so that you can supply the appropriate colors. Meanwhile, I shall take photographs. The black-and-white pictures, together with your color drawings, should provide quite an accurate portrayal. I was very pleasantly surprised by what I saw of your artistic abilities, my boy. Together we will accomplish much."

I could feel myself blushing from the unexpected praise. "I'll sure try, sir," I said, excited at the prospect of using colored paints.

"If you'd be so kind as to get the large canvas-wrapped pack I brought, perhaps we could get started now," he said.

Turning toward the house to get the pack, I realized I was beginning to feel better about my trip with Mr. Strawbridge. Maybe it would be interesting, after all.

"Your father will be wanting some lunch soon," Mama was saying when I returned. "Carrie, why don't you come on in the house with me while I fix something, and we'll let Tyler and Mr. Strawbridge get started here."

I decided to sketch the mangroves in ink first, the way I was used to doing. Then, I figured, I'd mix up the paints and add the color. I sat on the ground, trying to do my very best drawing, but trying, too, to watch Mr.

Strawbridge as he set up his camera. I heard him grumbling angrily to himself.

"Something wrong?" I asked.

He was holding the camera up to his face and looking through it, squinching up his eyes. "Damn the luck!" he said. Then, "Pardon my language, Tyler, but the camera lens is fogged with moisture. I'm afraid the salt water got into it somehow as I journeyed up the coast. I'm going to try leaving it here in the sun to see if it will dry out, but I'm not optimistic."

He fiddled with the camera some more, and finally set it on the ground with the lens facing the sun. Then he muttered, more to himself than to me, "With any luck, there'll be plenty of birds around, and the profits from this trip will buy a new camera, and a better one, at that."

I was about to ask him what he meant when he spoke directly to me again. "Without photographs, your drawings will be that much more important, young man. Let's see how you're doing there."

He came over and stood behind me. "That's very good, Tyler, very good indeed."

"Should I draw the little crabs and the snails, too, sir?" I asked. Looking so closely at the familiar trees was making me realize that mangroves were home to lots of smaller creatures. Small black crabs scuttled up and down the roots; spiraled tree snails clung to the leeward sides of the branches; butterflies hovered over the yellow flowers; and spiders hung from silken threads among the leaves. In the soft, oozy mud at the base of the roots, tiny shrimplike creatures hid from the brim and bass that poked around, feeding in the shallow water.

"Yes, Tyler, indeed. It would be excellent to show the role played by the seemingly humble mangrove in the lives of other—" Mr. Strawbridge stopped suddenly, uttering a loud gasp of surprise. He said, "Good Lord! Where on earth did he come from?"

I turned to see Mr. Strawbridge holding his hand over his heart. Standing behind him was Tommy. "Weren't you ever taught not to go around sneaking up on people?" Mr. Strawbridge asked indignantly. "You startled me!"

Tommy raised his eyebrows slightly, not understanding what Mr. Strawbridge was saying.

"Hey, Co-ooh-shee," I said, smiling at Tommy.

"Hel-lo, Ty-ler," he said.

Remembering my manners, I said, "Mr. Strawbridge, this is my friend Tommy Jumper. Co-ooh-shee's his real name." I pointed to Mr. Strawbridge and said his name slowly for Tommy.

I expected Mr. Strawbridge to say hello, but he ignored Tommy and spoke to me. "Jumper?" he repeated. "It was a Seminole by that name who showed me the way here."

"Right," I said. "That was Tommy's father."

"Interesting, isn't it, the English names they give themselves," he said.

Mama had called Mr. Strawbridge a cultured gentleman, and maybe he was, but it struck me as rude the way he was talking as if Tommy wasn't there, even though

55

Tommy couldn't understand the words. And he was staring at Tommy, studying him as if he were some unusual form of mangrove tree. I didn't bother to explain to him that Jumper was a name chosen by white traders who couldn't speak Miccosukee. Instead I held up my drawing and showed it to Tommy.

He reached for the drawing and ran his fingers over it, nodding his head up and down as he looked carefully at every detail. "Good," he said, handing it back to me. Then he reached into a pouch he wore under his shirt and brought out a small carving of a turtle. *"Yuk-chee,"* he said.

I repeated the word for "turtle" so I'd remember it. *"Yuk-chee."* I examined the carving, running my fingers over the smooth shell and the lifelike, sleepy-looking head. *"Hee-thee,"* I said, using the Miccosukee word for "good."

I'd taught Tommy about carving, and he liked to do it, too. We often showed each other what we'd made, and we had traded a few pieces back and forth. We'd spent many hours whittling together in the shade of the big palmetto tree, with just a few words passing between us.

Tommy said, *"Ish-kah-lof-kee?"* He held up his knife.

I felt Mr. Strawbridge jump beside me. "What's he doing with that knife?" he cried. His voice was high with alarm.

I laughed. "He's just asking if I want to do a little carving," I told Mr. Strawbridge.

Turning to Tommy, I said, *"He-ma-nee-ta-ko-tee-chee. Nee-tuck-cho-bee."* I pointed to Mr. Strawbridge. *"Co-na-*

wee." I pointed to myself. I hoped I was getting the words right. I was trying to explain that I'd be gone for many days with Mr. Strawbridge and that I was going to work for him.

Tommy looked away and frowned. I thought he was about to say something when Mama came out of the house.

"Hello, Tommy," she said. "We're about to sit down to some lunch. Would you like to join us?" She spoke in English, but as she did she made the motions for eating.

I'd noticed that the Seminoles didn't all sit down together for three meals a day, the way we did. There was always a big pot of stew or *ook-thee* hanging over the cooking fire in the middle of the village, and everyone helped themselves whenever they were hungry. But Tommy had never refused a meal when he'd been invited before, and I knew he understood what Mama was asking.

"Mama made biscuits, Tommy," Carrie said. Tommy liked Mama's biscuits a lot, especially when they were piled with jam. He definitely knew *that* word. But Tommy shook his head. *"Ah-thee-pa-lee,"* he said, and turned to leave.

I stood on the riverbank while Tommy pushed off in his canoe. As he started to pole upriver against the current, he looked back and said something that I didn't quite catch. I thought I heard the word *hum-pee*, but I wasn't sure, and the rest of what he said was drowned out by the sounds of the wind and the river.

I watched as Tommy's upright figure grew smaller and

smaller and finally disappeared around the bend. *Hum-pee* meant "bad," that much I knew. Was that what Tommy had said? And if so, *what* was bad? Frustrated, I shook my head, and went to tell Pa that we were ready to eat.

SEVEN

At Mama's urging, Mr. Strawbridge rested in the shade after lunch. Pa went back to his charcoal making, and Carrie came to watch me draw. I gave her some paper and one of the pens Mr. Strawbridge had brought, hoping he wouldn't mind. Carrie sat contentedly beside me, drawing large, friendly-looking butterflies with faces like people and practicing writing her name. I worked on the mangrove drawing, occasionally stopping to write a new word for Carrie to learn.

"Teach me a *big* word," she said.

Butterfly, I wrote. She liked that, and copied the letters carefully under mine.

"More," she demanded.

I wrote *mangrove.* That met with her approval, as did *Strawbridge.* She copied them both.

Crab, I wrote.

She made a face. "Too small."

I tried *alligator.*

She nodded happily and began writing, the tip of her tongue sticking out the side of her mouth as she concentrated on her work.

When I had sketched a large clump of mangroves as well as I could, I reached for the tubes of paint Mr. Strawbridge had given me. I chose green first, to color in the leaves, but the color was wrong. Too bright. I experimented, adding some blue and some yellow and some red until it looked right to me. I painted a few leaves and, comparing what I'd painted to the real ones, discovered that the actual leaves were all slightly different in color. This was going to be more complicated than I'd thought.

Carrie wanted to color in her butterflies, but Mama's voice carried from the garden. "Carrie, you leave Mr. Strawbridge's things alone."

Carrie's lip quivered as she looked longingly at the bright tubes of color, and I whispered, "When Mr. Strawbridge pays me, we'll go straight to Storter's store and buy us some paints of our own."

"Really, Ty?" she asked.

"Sure," I said. "And a real pad of paper like this, not just wrinkly old wrapping paper."

"And a knife like yours?" she asked slyly.

I laughed and tussled her gently to the ground. "You never give up, do you?"

Carrie rolled on the ground, shrieking as I tickled her under her arms. When I was starting on the bottoms of her feet, her most tickly place, a movement near the river caught my eye. "Bean!" I cried. I jumped up, Carrie right behind me, and we ran to the water's edge, where Bean Thompson was landing his little flat-bottomed skiff.

"Hey, Bean," we called.

"Hey, yourselves," he said, grinning his wide-open, snaggletoothed smile. "I'd swear I heard the most god-awful screeching coming from around these parts. Sounded like a shark-bit soprano."

"It was me!" Carrie cried. "Tyler's the shark!"

Then Carrie and I both began talking at once. We were awfully glad to see Bean, and eager to tell him the news about Mr. Strawbridge coming and the trip I was going to take. Bean laughed and tried to listen to the two of us at the same time. I ran to get my drawing to show him, and Carrie, not to be outdone, got her paper, too, and stuck it under Bean's nose.

Pointing to each word as he said it aloud, he pretended to read very slowly what Carrie had written: "Bean, please stay and eat dinner with us." He looked up at Carrie, his eyes wide. "Why, I hadn't planned on it, missy, but since you asked so nice and all, well, I reckon I just might could!"

"Bean! That's not what it says!" Carrie protested, but Bean scooped her up and swung her onto his shoulders while he studied my drawing. "It looks mighty real, Tyler," he said. "But what, if you'll pardon me for asking, do you want to go drawing a bunch of mangroves for? If you want to see mangroves, all you have to do is open your eyes."

I was starting to explain when Mama stuck her head out the door. "My, my," she said, "if that's Bean Thompson, then it must be getting on time for dinner." She was raising her eyebrows and trying hard to look stern.

"I hadn't hardly noticed the time myself, ma'am," said Bean. "But I did catch a mess of brim today, and I'd be happy to share 'em. Could you maybe fry 'em up in some of that cornmeal batter you make so good?" he asked hopefully.

Mama smiled. "Of course, Bean. Tyler, why don't you go get your pa and tell him Bean's here. Carrie, you wake up Mr. Strawbridge, and, Bean, as soon as you clean those fish I'll get started frying them."

I ran to get Pa, glad to be bringing some good news this time.

It felt like a party, what with Bean and Mr. Strawbridge both for company. There was talk and fooling at dinner such as I could hardly remember. Pa was in better spirits than the night before. Bean always seemed to have that effect on folks, making them happier than they'd felt before he showed up, wiggling his eyebrows and smiling in that lopsided way he had.

We packed away a pile of food. Bean filled his plate at least three times before pushing it away, saying, "Now that, I believe, was the best darn fish fry I've ever had the pleasure of eating, Mary."

"Why, thank you, Bean," said Mama.

Mr. Strawbridge set down his napkin, leaned back in his chair, and said, "Mrs. MacCauley, I, too, must compliment you on the preparation of this meal. It was what can only be described as a piscatory delight." He rubbed his belly and beamed at Mama.

Bean's eyes got real big. "Say what?"

"What's the matter, Bean?" asked Pa with a grin. "Don't you agree with Mr. Strawbridge's opinion of Mary's cooking?"

"I might," answered Bean, "if I knew what the devil he said."

"Piscatory," repeated Mr. Strawbridge. " 'Of or relating to fish or fishing.' "

Pa grinned wickedly at Bean. "So what the man means, Bean, is that Mary makes a darn good fish fry."

Bean looked at Carrie and me, his eyes wide and innocent. "Now, didn't I just say that?" he asked.

Pa laughed uproariously, and Carrie and I hid our smiles behind our hands. Even Mama's lips were twitching, but Mr. Strawbridge didn't seem to notice that the joke was on him. He asked Bean, "And what is it that you do, Mr. Thompson?"

Bean looked amused. "Well, now, Mr. Strawbridge, I guess you could say I do what I like. I hunt and fish to eat. I trade for tools and tobacco from time to time. I got no need for money. And except for these fine folks here, I guess you could say I prefer the company of the skeeters to that of most people I've run into."

"I see," said Mr. Strawbridge with a lift of his eyebrows. I could tell that Bean's easygoing ways struck Mr. Strawbridge as peculiar.

Bean turned to me. "Now, Tyler, why don't you tell me about this expedition you're goin' on."

"Well," I began eagerly, "Mr. Strawbridge wants me to

show him all the different kinds of plants and animals and birds, and we'll draw them and take photographs of them and—"

"I'm afraid we won't be taking any pictures," Mr. Strawbridge said, interrupting. "The camera did not take kindly to its dose of salt water. I'll be relying heavily on Tyler's drawings to create a record of what we see."

"Where are you headed?" Bean asked.

I looked at Mr. Strawbridge. "You're the guide," he said.

I hadn't thought yet about where we'd go. "Up Lostman's, I guess," I said, "and back into the bays."

"In two weeks you could get all the way up to Chokoloskee and back," suggested Bean. "You know the way?"

"I guess," I said, though I wasn't really sure. I'd only been once with Pa, when we took the backwater route to the store, something Pa had vowed never to do again. We'd just about choked on the skeeters.

"You'll want to stay out of the way of the plumers," Bean advised.

Mr. Strawbridge smiled. "I daresay they are a dastardly bunch, from what I've heard, but surely they would respect the fact that my work is of a scientific nature."

Bean hooted. "All they respect is the point of a gun," he said. "And the prospect of a dollar."

"But surely the laws against pluming have thinned the numbers of hunters somewhat," said Mr. Strawbridge.

Bean hooted again. "Mr. Strawbridge," he said, "those

laws have only made the plumers more wily than ever."

"Nevertheless," said Mr. Strawbridge, "I find it hard to believe that—"

"Let me tell you a little story, sir," said Bean, "and then you can tell me what you do or don't believe."

Carrie and I leaned forward. We loved listening to Bean's stories.

"Less than one year ago," Bean began, "let's see, it'll be a year this coming July, I guess, plume hunters killed a man by the name of Guy Bradley down near Oyster Key."

I leaned forward in my seat. I'd heard some talk about Bradley's murder, but I was anxious to hear the whole story.

"Now, this fellow Bradley had lived down near Flamingo most all of his life," Bean continued, "and had done his share of plume bird shooting himself, starting when he was just a tyke younger than Tyler here. But the way I heard it, he began to notice as the years went by that there weren't so many birds as there used to be in these parts, and he figured he knew the reason. So when the first laws against pluming were passed— Just when exactly was that, Will?"

"Few years ago," Pa answered. "Around 1901 or thereabouts."

"I believe you're right. So, anyway," Bean went on, "when Bradley heard about the regulations against pluming, he became a regular convert to the law. Now, the law is something most folks around here aren't exactly on speaking terms with, if you see what I'm saying. They thought the whole idea was a joke. Figured they were going to keep on doing what they'd always done, and who was going to stop 'em? Figured they'd make their own laws, same as always. Some big shot somewhere saying pluming's a crime didn't make it a crime to them. It's just a way to make a living."

Pa was nodding his head in agreement.

"Well," said Bean, "when word got out and about that the Audubons—that's them Yankee bird lovers—"

"I am familiar with the work of the Audubon Society," said Mr. Strawbridge.

"Oh. So you knew they hired Bradley on as the first 'game warden,' as they called it," said Bean.

"No, sir, I didn't," said Mr. Strawbridge. "Please go on with your story."

"Yeah. So Bradley heard that the Audubons wanted to hire someone to protect the rookeries and enforce the laws, and he figured he was the man for the job. He knew the plumers' ways, you see, and he had what you might call some righteous indignation built up concerning the issue. Now, mind you, Bradley wasn't the sort to go around talking big about being a warden. He was a quiet type. Quiet, but tough as a gator's hide.

"Word spread, of course, the way it does, and Guy was suddenly a man without a whole lot of friends. He did his job, though, and found out quick enough that, often as not, being a warden meant getting shot at and threatened by the plumers."

Mama began shifting in her chair. I could see she was getting nervous about the way the talk was headed, and I thought she probably wouldn't want Carrie hearing talk of murder and the like. She stood up, saying, "Excuse me, Bean, but I think Carrie and I'll excuse ourselves. Come on, Carrie, come with Mama, and we'll go read us our own story."

Carrie frowned. "But I want to hear *this* story." Her face was beginning to gather into an expression that meant a serious ruckus was coming.

Pa must have seen it, too, because he said, "Carrie, honey, go on with your mama now. Bean will come say good night to you before he leaves, won't you, Bean?"

"I wouldn't leave without telling Carrie a certain story I made up just for her," declared Bean. "And it's not some tired old story about a bunch of plume hunters, either."

The corners of Carrie's mouth turned up in the tiniest hint of a smile.

"And no one's to listen but Carrie, y'all understand?" Bean told the rest of us.

Carrie smirked at me with satisfaction, got up, and followed Mama to our room, where Mama or Pa often read out loud to us at night.

"Thanks, Bean," said Pa.

"Don't mention it. Now, where was I? Oh yeah, so there was one family in particular who was getting under Bradley's skin. A plumer by the name of Walter Smith and his sons were flaunting the law openly, not even trying to be sneaky about it the way most folks were, and

67

Guy arrested one son, Tom, twice. A risky business, when you think about it, arresting men with guns in their hands. Whereupon the old man, Walter, announced to all the world that if Guy Bradley tried to arrest him or any of his family again, Walter would kill him.

"Well, like I said, they were just as bold as could be. So one day they sailed their schooner out to the Oyster Key rookery, went ashore, and began shooting egrets. Mind you, Oyster Key sits just a little over a mile across the water from where Bradley lived at Flamingo. There was no question he'd hear the shots. And, sure enough, Guy got in his skiff and headed out to the Smiths' schooner, where they had taken their kill of birds. I guess you could say that what happened after that will never be fully known, because Bradley's not around to tell his side of the story. But the next day, Guy's brother found Guy lying in a pool of blood in the bottom of his skiff, which had washed into shore and caught in some mangroves. He was dead."

We were all quiet for a moment. Then Mr. Strawbridge said, "If this is common knowledge, Mr. Thompson, then surely the culprit was dealt with summarily in a court of law."

Bean just looked at Mr. Strawbridge from under his eyebrows and kept talking. "Smith turned himself in to the authorities in Key West, claiming he shot Bradley in self-defense, and there was a grand jury investigation. Now, everybody knew Smith had threatened to kill Bradley. And the Audubon folks dug up all kinds of evidence to show Bradley'd been murdered. For instance, they proved that Guy's gun had never even been fired."

"So this murdering scoundrel Smith was found guilty and sent to jail," finished Mr. Strawbridge.

"I'm afraid you're wrong, Mr. Strawbridge," said Bean. "The Monroe County grand jury voted not to indict Walter Smith. He's a free man."

"That's not fair!" I burst out.

Bean shrugged. "Depends on your point of view, I guess. Some folks saw it as justice." Turning to Mr. Strawbridge, he said, "So, like I said, stay out of the way of the plumers. The Audubons have tried to get another man to fill Bradley's shoes, but so far no one's been too eager for the position. I'd wager that the plumers are feeling pretty cocky these days."

Mr. Strawbridge swallowed, then nodded.

I was glad Mama hadn't been listening. So far, she'd been happy about the idea of my going with Mr. Strawbridge, and I didn't want her to start fretting.

"Bean," I said, "plume hunters have got no reason to bother with us, anyhow. This is a scientific expedition, not a hunting trip. Isn't that right, Mr. Strawbridge?"

Mr. Strawbridge looked down at the front of his white shirt and wiped at a spot that I couldn't see. He kept his eyes down on his shirtfront as he answered, "Of course."

I smiled at Bean, but he didn't smile back. He was still looking at Mr. Strawbridge. It seemed that Bean was waiting for Mr. Strawbridge to say something else, but Mr. Strawbridge was still concerning himself with the front of his shirt and appeared, for once, to have nothing more to say.

"Speaking of plumers, Bean," said Pa, "I had a fellow named Brewer stop by here the other day. He was looking to find the Alfords to do some pluming for some New York City outfit. Tried to sign me up while he was at it."

"What did you tell him?" Bean asked.

"You know how I feel about that," Pa answered.

"I got no use for it, either," said Bean, "but I could understand if you'd felt you had to do it, a man with a family like you've got here."

Mr. Strawbridge looked up suddenly and changed the subject. "Need we be concerned about savages?" he asked.

"Savages?" Bean repeated.

"Seminoles," Mr. Strawbridge said, sounding somewhat impatient. "This afternoon, Tyler's acquaintance, the Jumper lad, pulled out a knife, and it occurred to me that—" He stopped when he saw our astonished faces.

"You don't have to worry about the Seminoles," Pa said shortly. "Didn't Tommy's father bring you here safe and sound?"

"I told you Tommy took out his knife to see if I wanted to do some wood carving," I said. "What did you think he was going to do?" The idea that Mr. Strawbridge had been afraid of Tommy was ridiculous.

"You'll find," said Bean quietly, "that the Seminoles don't want to see you any more than you want to see them." Then, turning from Mr. Strawbridge to Pa and me, he said, "Now, who's ready to get whupped at cards?"

"I'm not much of a gambler myself," Mr. Strawbridge was saying when Mama's voice called from the other room. "There's a sleepy girl in here who'd like to hear just one more story," she said. "And then I think it would be a good idea for all of us to turn in. Tyler, you and Mr. Strawbridge will be leaving early tomorrow. Wouldn't you like to get a good night's sleep?"

I'd much rather stay up and play cards with Bean, I thought, but I didn't say it out loud. When Mama asked a question like that, she didn't really want an answer. It looked as if the party was over.

Later, as I lay awake in bed, I thought about going with Mr. Strawbridge in the morning. I still couldn't decide how I felt about it, or about him. I'd felt proud when he praised my drawing, and excited about all the things he could teach me. I liked the way he was always asking questions about things, like how mangroves could drink salt water. It was something I'd never asked myself. I felt good, too, about earning money to buy paints for Carrie and a new dress or a sewing machine for Mama. Maybe Pa would be able to take a break from the drudgery of cutting buttonwood.

Why, then, did I feel a strange uneasiness in the pit of my stomach?

EIGHT

Pa and I finished loading the canoe just after sunup. The provisions Mr. Strawbridge had brought, the small sack containing my clothes, and another sack of food Mama had added were all stowed where they'd stay safe and dry. There was nothing else to do but say good-bye. Carrie surprised me by wrapping her arms around my legs and crying, saying she didn't want me to go. The sight of her tearstained face made my own throat start to close up, although I wasn't sure why. I picked her up and swung her high over my head, the way she liked me to do, and told her I'd be back before she knew it.

I'd thought Mama was all for my going on this trip, but her face had a funny, crumply look as she hugged me. "Make me proud, Ty," she said. Then she added in a whisper, "And—be careful."

"I will, Mama," I promised.

Then Pa was shaking my hand and saying, "You've got a good head on your shoulders, son. If you get into trouble, use it."

"Yes, sir," I said.

Mr. Strawbridge got into the canoe and perched awkwardly in the front, on top of the sack that held my clothes. I stood in the back, ready to start poling upriver, having already decided that we'd both be better-off if Mr. Strawbridge let me do the navigating. He might know a lot about science and the like, but I'd already seen how little he knew about practical matters like handling a boat.

Mr. Strawbridge called, "I'll bring the boy back safely in two weeks' time, Mrs. MacCauley, richer, I hope, in all ways from his experience."

Mama smiled and waved as we pushed off from shore. Pa picked up Carrie and held her while she, too, waved good-bye. I couldn't wave 'cause of holding on to the pole, but I gave a long look back at my family. Seeing them standing there, saying good-bye, gave me a peculiar sharp feeling in my chest, and I had to fight a sudden urge to turn right around and go home. Then we came to a bend in the river and Pa, Mama, and Carrie disappeared from sight. Shaking my head, I told myself to stop being silly and concentrate on the job at hand.

I poled along the familiar waters, figuring Mr. Strawbridge would let me know if he wanted to stop, and soon he did. We passed a large key that had a stand of black mangroves growing on it, and he asked me to pull up. We spent a couple of hours there. I drew the trees, while Mr. Strawbridge examined the roots and the soil around the trees. Then he measured the leaves and the height of the branches, and took samples of everything, which he placed in special, carefully marked little envelopes.

After we ate some of Mama's biscuits and jelly, we pushed off and headed upriver. "Well, Mr. Strawbridge," I asked, "what is it you'd like to see next?" I was anxious on this first day to show Mr. Strawbridge that I was going to be a good guide, worth three dollars a day, at least.

"One of my primary interests, Tyler," he answered, "is to study various bird species. What I've been longing to see is a rookery, with nesting birds in the full glory of the mating season."

"I know a place like that," I said proudly.

"You do?" asked Mr. Strawbridge, looking excited.

"Sure," I answered. "My friend Tommy showed it to . . ." My voice faded as I remembered my promise to Tommy.

The rookery was our secret. "No *ah-poh-nee-kee yat-hot-kee*." Don't tell any white man, Tommy had said. And I had promised.

"But I—I said I wouldn't tell anybody about it," I mumbled. "I promised."

Mr. Strawbridge was staring at me, a look of disappointment on his face.

"I'll find us another rookery, sir," I offered hopefully. "There's plenty of birds around, you wait and see."

"Tyler," said Mr. Strawbridge, "I appreciate that you are a young man of your word, but surely your friend Tommy would not mind your showing *me* the rookery. After all, I am a scientist. And you were hired on, you remember, to share with me your knowledge of this area. I'm paying you very good money to do just that, as I'm sure you are aware. If you do your job well, that is."

Listening to Mr. Strawbridge was getting me mixed up. I'd promised Tommy to keep the rookery a secret, but Mr. Strawbridge was making it sound as if I was breaking my agreement with *him* if I *didn't* take him to the rookery. I didn't want him to be sorry he'd picked me for his guide. Mama and Pa were counting on me to earn three dollars a day. And Mr. Strawbridge *was* a scientist, as he'd said.

"Well, Tyler?" Mr. Strawbridge asked.

"I don't know," I said. "I wish I'd known you wanted to go there. I could have asked Tommy about it yesterday."

Mr. Strawbridge smiled. "He won't ever have to know we were there, Tyler, unless you tell him."

I frowned.

"Or, perhaps," he said, "you could give Tommy some of the money you earn to smooth things over."

I looked at him, thinking maybe he wasn't so smart, after all. I'd still have broken my promise, whether Tommy found out about it or not. And giving him money wouldn't change anything.

"Tyler, I'm anxious to see that rookery. Will you take me there or not? I'll find another guide if I need to, one who understands and appreciates the importance of my work." He paused. "I'd prefer not to, you know," he went on. "Your mother was so pleased at the prospect of our working together."

Mr. Strawbridge was looking at me impatiently. I felt foolish. I wasn't some dumb backwoods kid who couldn't understand about science. Here I had my first chance to do something grown-up and important. I wasn't going to back out of it.

"All right," I said, pushing hard on the pole, as if to convince myself that I was headed in the right direction. "Let's go."

After we had poled for several hours, following the narrow channels that Tommy had shown me, the clamor of the rookery began to fill our ears. I couldn't help smiling at the sound of it, and at the prospect of seeing all those birds and their babies once again.

I'd been watchful all day, but became especially wary as we got close to the nesting grounds, looking and listening for signs of hunters. Bean's story was fresh in my mind, and I couldn't help remembering others I'd heard about the treachery of the plumers: how they'd remove channel markers or set up fake ones to keep other hunters from finding "their" rookery; or even fell a bunch of trees across a waterway to keep folks away from their spot; how they'd kill a man they didn't know just on the chance that he was the law, or another hunter come to shoot "their" birds.

But the peaceful activity of the rookery was just as it had been when I'd come with Tommy, except that showers had fallen over the past few days and had made the water a few inches higher. I was able to pole the canoe quietly right up to the edge of the nesting grounds. There, once again, was the noisy, bustling spectacle of hundreds of birds going about the business of mating and raising their young.

Mr. Strawbridge sat for several moments, just watching, and I thought I saw on his face some of the same feeling of awe that I'd first felt at the sight, and was feeling all over again. I expected that soon we'd get to work, doing whatever scientific stuff he wanted to do, but for a moment we just watched. I hoped that Mr. Strawbridge would tell me to get out the drawing paper and pens. I wondered how I'd mix a color that would match the delicate pink of the rosy spoonbill's feathers, or the darker pink that flashed when it lifted its wings to preen. I couldn't wait to try.

I turned to ask Mr. Strawbridge if he wanted to pull up on the shore, or if we'd work from the boat. He was fumbling in one of the packs. To my amazement, he pulled out a gun. Dumbly I watched him load it. Before I could find my voice to ask what he was doing, he stood up, took aim, and began to shoot: *Blam! Blam! Blam-blam!*

At the sound of the gun, hundreds of birds took to the air. The world was suddenly filled with the sounds of their startled cries and the beating of their wings.

Blam! Blam-blam! Blam!

I lost track of how many times Mr. Strawbridge shot. The blasting of the gun was almost lost in the awful confusion and uproar as the birds, panic-stricken, flew in all directions.

I stood, stunned, as the squawking of the birds slowly died away, leaving a stillness and silence like the end of the world.

The quiet was broken by Mr. Strawbridge's triumphant cry: "Ah-ha!" He turned to me excitedly and said, "Quickly, Tyler, let's retrieve them and see what we've got."

Still in a daze, I poled the canoe along and, one by one, picked up the dead, floating birds and threw them in the bottom of the boat. Mr. Strawbridge examined each one, stretching its wings out and feeling it all over. "Splendid specimens," he proclaimed. "Tonight I'll show you my method for preserving the hides. That will be one of your daily duties, of course. Now let us proceed. We won't be getting any more birds from here today."

"That's for sure," I muttered to myself as Mr. Strawbridge settled himself back onto the sack of clothing, and I began to pole mechanically, I didn't know where. I felt confused and furious. And stupid.

My mind was spinning. He had tricked me. He'd tricked us all. All his talk about collecting specimens. He'd never said he meant *dead* ones! He had praised my talent for art, talking about how I'd be drawing plants and animals so that people could see what they looked like. Never had he mentioned killing birds. A scientific expedition, he'd said, not a hunting trip. When he talked me into showing him Tommy's and my secret place, I never dreamed he would kill the birds we found there. And, I thought wildly, who would have thought the little man would be such a good shot, anyway?

Surely Mama and Pa hadn't understood what Mr. Strawbridge had planned to do. All his big talk must have muddled up their brains the way it had mine.

When I could trust my voice, I said, "Just what kind of scientific business was that? Are you going to be shooting everything we see?"

Mr. Strawbridge turned to look at me and sighed. "Why don't you take us in to shore, Tyler, and we'll have us a little talk," he said. "I haven't fully explained the aims of this undertaking to you, I suppose. It's time to stop, anyway, and set up camp. I will try this evening to further elucidate our mission."

I poled in silence until I saw the high ground of an old shell mound, and I pulled up to make camp. The mounds were places where the Indians called Calusas, who'd lived in these parts even before the Seminoles, had made their homes. They'd picked spots that were above the waterline and made them even higher with the shells of all the clams and turtles and oysters they ate. Thanks to those fish-eating Indians, we'd have a dry place to spend the night.

Without speaking to Mr. Strawbridge, I began looking for dry wood to start a fire. He was rummaging through the packs, taking out his notebooks and pens and all sorts of gadgets, and spreading them on a canvas sheet. Once the fire was crackling, I took two of the skinned birds and set them to cooking on a stick. I sat with my back to Mr. Strawbridge, staring blindly at the fire. After a while he came over, sat down near me, and began to talk.

"It takes money to pay for scientific expeditions such as this, Tyler, surely you realize that. I had to travel here from New York. I had to buy this canoe, these packs, these provisions, the paints, the camera. I have to pay you." He paused, and I looked away. "Museums pay me handsomely for the specimens I can provide: hides, eggs, feathers, what-have-you. So in answer to your question, yes, we will be collecting whatever we can. Some of these birds, for instance," he said, pointing to the carcasses in the bottom of the boat, "will be stuffed and displayed in places such as the Smithsonian Institution. Some of the plumes will be sold to cover my expenses. I'll need to buy a new camera. Do you know what that will cost?"

How would I know? I didn't care, either.

"Tyler," he said, "do you have any idea what the future holds for this place you call home?"

I shrugged, wondering what that had to do with anything. "Things don't change much around here except for going from dry season to wet season and back again," I said.

"Oh, but that is where you are wrong, Tyler," said Mr. Strawbridge. "The winds of change are always blowing, and they are finally reaching way down to this untouched corner of the world. Why, even as we speak, your Governor Broward's dredges are digging canals through the Everglades, draining away the water that flows through them, the water that provides life for all the birds and fish and mammals and smaller creatures. And why? Because he wants people to come here, Tyler, to farm the land and build settlements and grow rich."

"But no one down here is rich," I said, frowning. What

was he talking about? "And Mama says no folks with sense want to come here at all."

"She's right, son. Most folks don't. They don't want to come here the way it is. Right now this is a wilderness. But there are people who want to transform the face of the land, Tyler, to make it *civilized*, so that they'll feel comfortable here."

"You mean make it into cities like up north?" I asked, trying to picture it.

"That's right," said Mr. Strawbridge.

"But they can't," I said. "There's alligators and plume birds and panthers and sea turtles and skeeters and miles and miles of water here. There's nothing like this in New York!"

"Tyler," said Mr. Strawbridge, "you'd be surprised to know how much of a wilderness New York once was, not so very long ago. You see, where people go, their needs and desires come first. Alligators, plume birds, panthers, mosquitoes—they have no place in civilization.

"And so, Tyler, my mission is to gather specimens of the creatures who live here before they are gone, so that we will have some sort of scientific record of their existence. When the time comes that we can no longer see these magnificent creatures in their natural habitat, we will at least be able to examine their remains, stuffed and mounted in museums, or to enjoy their likeness in drawings such as those done by Mr. Audubon."

I looked around me at the sky and the river and the mangroves that hid the wild creatures and kept their secrets. The sky and water and trees seemed never to end. Nor did there seem to be any end to all the different kinds of life. We'd just seen a rookery spilling over with birds.

Mr. Strawbridge's words made no sense. Why, this place was so far from civilization that Mama never felt the end of despair about it. And, besides, if Mr. Strawbridge was so worried about a time when there weren't any birds left, how come he'd just shot a bunch of them?

As if he'd read my mind, he said, "Between the dredging and the hunters, I'm afraid the days of the plume birds are coming to an end, just as the days of the dinosaurs had to end. In the face of that, Tyler, is what I did this afternoon really so terrible?"

Was it? I didn't know. How much of what he'd said was true? It seemed to me that in Mr. Strawbridge's mind the dredges had already drained away all the water, cities had been built up, and the wild creatures were all gone, save for those he had shot and stuffed.

Supper was quiet. Mr. Strawbridge left me alone while I tried to sort out what he'd been saying. Something was bothering me. It was like a skeeter buzzing in my ear that wouldn't go away. Mr. Strawbridge had lots of book learning, anybody could tell that. And he sure knew more than I did about what was going on in the big world far from Lostman's River. But if he hadn't actually lied straight out about what we were going to be doing, he sure had held back some of the truth of it. And as far as I was concerned, that meant he was hardly the perfect gentleman Mama thought he was.

After we ate, Mr. Strawbridge showed me how to pre-pare the hides of the dead birds, and I found myself inter-ested in spite of my anger. Using a small scale and ruler, he weighed and measured each bird and recorded the numbers in a log. He had shot seven white herons, six egrets, three cormorants, two Louisiana herons, two flamingos, five pelicans, a spoonbill, and four of what we called ironheads and he called wood ibis. The measuring and recording took quite a long time.

Then Mr. Strawbridge showed me how he wanted the skins of the birds to be preserved. I watched him and, using my knife, did the same. Starting about halfway up the neck, we skinned down to the tail, taking all the skin off the body clear out to the first joint of the wing. Then we mixed up some lime and water in a gallon can Mr. Strawbridge had brought along. We stretched out the skins with the feathers down, painted the skin side with the limewater, rubbed them with cornmeal, and stretched them out with little sticks to dry.

Mr. Strawbridge said they'd last a long time that way, long enough for him to ship them to Paris and London, where, he told me, he got anywhere from fifty cents for a pelican skin to twenty-five dollars for the skin of a flamin-go! He was especially happy that we'd gotten two of the big pink birds because there were hardly any of them left. And then there was the money he'd get for the plumes from the egrets and herons.

When we had finished preparing the specimens, I pointed to the pile of skinned birds. "What should I do with all those?" I asked.

I figured he'd tell me to salt the meat or cook it up now to eat later when we needed it. To my surprise, he said, "Get rid of them, Ty. We'll have fresh meat tomorrow. But throw them over there"—he gestured behind him, toward the riverbank—"so we don't have varmints coming around here tonight, scavenging."

I did what Mr. Strawbridge told me to do, but I felt terrible about it. I knew what Pa would think of such waste. Pa was like an Indian that way. He didn't shoot what he didn't need for food, and he wouldn't throw out meat that was perfectly good for eating. I knew how he felt about shooting birds just for their feathers. Now I wondered what he'd think about killing them for Mr. Strawbridge's purposes. For scientific knowledge. It made me feel downright peculiar. As I set the bird carcasses down by the river, I felt my cheeks flush with the shame of it.

I set up the tents on the driest ground, making sure to look around for snakes. Then, glad to be done with Mr. Strawbridge and his talk, I crawled under my blanket.

Even tired as I was, sleep was a long time coming. I lay in the tent, listening to the rain dripping on the roof and the sounds of the night animals: the hoot of an owl, the shriek of a panther, and later, a splashing and crunching down by the river. Slipping out of the tent, I lit the lantern and went to investigate. There on the shore was a huge alligator eating the remains of the birds. The gator seemed frozen in the light from the lantern, its eyes gleaming above the surface of the water.

I'd heard about hunters jacklighting gators, and now I

could see how easy it would be to shoot out an entire gator hole in one night using a light. I blew out the lantern and went back to bed.

Somehow it made me feel better, knowing somebody had gotten a good meal off those birds.

NINE

The weather turned cold during the night, and I woke up shivering. I stuck my head out of the tent to find that a light drizzle was falling, and I crawled back under the blanket again. I knew I was supposed to get up, start the fire, and get something cooking for breakfast. But for a moment I lay back, wishing I was waking up in my own bed at home, with Carrie snuffling awake in the bed next to me, Pa getting the stove going, and Mama stirring up some of her biscuits. I felt so homesick I almost thought I'd cry, and I quick jumped out of the tent so as not to think about it anymore.

I put on my waterproof coat and began looking around for some dry wood to start a fire with, promising myself that from then on I'd take some wood into the tent with me at night. When the fire was crackling and I had the coffee started, Mr. Strawbridge came out of his tent. He stretched, sniffed the air, and began talking.

"I realize, Tyler, that you were somewhat dismayed by yesterday's events."

I shrugged and stirred cornmeal into the pot of boiling water. Let him talk if he wants to, I told myself.

"Did you know that John James Audubon himself considered it a poor day's work when he shot fewer than one hundred birds?" he asked. "He never did his drawings from stuffed specimens, only from freshly killed birds, which he posed to look natural. And Audubon's name is now associated with bird preservation, as mine will be someday. My contributions to the collections of museums around the world will be unparalleled. Someday the Strawbridge name will be cloaked in all the glory that has been visited upon the name of Audubon."

I looked at the way Mr. Strawbridge's face got all dreamy-looking, just thinking about having the "glory" of this fellow Audubon.

The name Audubon made me think about Guy Bradley, the warden who had been murdered trying to enforce the laws against shooting plume birds. I had clean forgotten that plume hunting was against the law, common as it was.

"You're shooting plume birds," I blurted. "Aren't you breaking the law, same as the other hunters?"

Mr. Strawbridge's face had turned bright red from the sun the day before. Now it grew even redder, and his chin shook with what I took to be indignation at my question. "The purposes of Hugo M. Strawbridge are entirely honorable, young man," he said, "and are at odds with those of the plume hunters who kill purely from greed, with no appreciation whatsoever of the majesty of the creatures they slaughter. Why, Tyler, surely you can see the difference between killing birds for money and killing them in order that they may be preserved for the furthering of scientific knowledge. Why, compared to the kind of wholesale slaughter going on down here, the few birds I shoot are hardly worth mentioning."

"But you get paid, same as they do," I said, puzzled. "You said you get money for every skin. And look at all the plume birds you shot. You get money for those feathers, same as the other hunters."

"Ahhh," he said, "but my motives are different. I seek payment only to cover the expense of my expeditions. Let me remind you that trips such as this cost money, Tyler."

"But," I went on, "what I meant was, aren't we breaking the law, just like those hunters?"

"The goals to which I am committed are above the bounds of laws made by well-meaning, but misinformed, individuals," said Mr. Strawbridge. "And I believe we have said quite enough about the subject for one morning. Pack up the canoe now, and let's be on our way."

Miserably I took down the tents and stowed our gear in the canoe. I was wondering how I could feel worse than I did at that moment when Mr. Strawbridge announced, "Take me to the rookery again, Tyler, and we'll see what we find today."

"Mr. Strawbridge, sir," I said, "I don't much want to go back there. You know, because of my promise and all. I'll find you some more birds someplace else, you'll see."

Mr. Strawbridge's face didn't change. His voice, always so polite and gentlemanly, didn't change, either. He smiled at me from under his bushy eyebrows and spoke real slowly, as if I were simpleminded, or hard-of-hearing. "We've been through this before, Tyler. I thought you understood. You were hired to do my bidding, not to question my decisions. And what I wish to do is return to the rookery. Now, shall we proceed?"

As I poled the canoe, I thought of all the things I could do. I could take us up one dead-end creek after another and pretend that I couldn't find the rookery. I could pull up to some place for lunch and leave Mr. Strawbridge stranded there. That would show him! Or I'd simply head for home and put an end to this trip once and for all. He probably wouldn't even notice we were headed in the wrong direction until it was too late.

In my mind I saw the disappointment on Carrie's face when I told her there would be no new paints, after all. I heard Pa's voice saying that a little extra money would help to ease some of Mama's burden. How could I return empty-handed?

I pointed the canoe in the direction of the rookery.

Everything happened pretty much the way it had the day before. Mr. Strawbridge shot eight big white herons, a dozen small ones, nine egrets, two curlews, a man-o'-war bird, and five pelicans.

When we left there, I followed the river upstream a while to where a small creek broke off to the east. It was getting toward sundown, so I found us a place to camp on an island. There was a grove of cabbage palms about a hundred yards west of the creek that would give good shelter.

I set off to collect firewood, and Mr. Strawbridge was

commencing to prepare the bird skins. As I started back to camp with the wood, four canoes appeared around the bend. I looked over at Mr. Strawbridge, hoping to catch his eye and signal him to hush. We didn't know who these men were. They looked to me like plumers, and it was best not to ask for trouble. But Mr. Strawbridge was already waving foolishly, stepping out of the cover of the palms and over to the creek.

My heart lurched in my chest as I saw one of the men in the lead canoe draw his rifle and point it at Mr. Strawbridge.

"Good evening, gentlemen," Mr. Strawbridge called, unaware of the gun pointing in his direction. "Might I inquire as to whether you've seen many plume birds in the course of your travels?"

"You might," said the man with the gun. He laughed, and the sound of it gave me a shiver down my back. "But you won't be around to hear the answer."

He looked down the barrel of his gun, and, before I could take in what was happening, surely before Mr. Strawbridge had time to understand his mistake, the man fired.

With horror, I watched Mr. Strawbridge's small body fall backward to the ground. His head shook once or twice from side to side, as if he were trying to say, "No, no, no. . . ." He twitched a few times and then lay still.

The man with the gun signalled for the other canoes to pull in to shore. There were eight men. By that time all of them had drawn their guns, and eight pairs of eyes searched our camp.

"Look around," ordered the man who had shot. "I'll bet Mr. Fancypants isn't alone out here."

I must have dropped to the ground at the sound of the shot, dumping my load of wood, without even realizing I'd done it. I was pretty well hidden behind some scrubby brush, but if the men really looked, they'd find me for sure. Desperately I looked around. Behind me was what was left of a burned Indian dugout, overturned on the ground. I crawled underneath the hollowed-out log canoe, thankful for the darkness that was coming on fast now, and lay still, listening.

One of the men was very close. I could hear him stamping around, kicking at the underbrush. With my eyes closed, I prayed that he wouldn't stumble upon the firewood I'd dropped and become suspicious. I prayed, too, that the pounding of my heart wasn't as loud as it sounded to me. How could the man not hear it! The air seemed filled with the echo of my wild fear: *Please don't find me please don't kill me please don't find me please don't kill me please don't please don't please please please. . .*

I don't know how long I lay there, utterly still, waiting for the dugout to be turned over, for a sneering voice to call, "Here he is, boys," and for another shot to fill the night with sound. Long after the footsteps had faded away, I remained, unable to move.

Finally some distant part of my brain understood that the men had decided Mr. Strawbridge was alone, after all. That faraway part of my mind was grateful that I hadn't already set up the two tents, which would have alerted the men that I was around someplace. They had given up searching for me and were making camp. I could hear their voices faintly as they shouted back and forth to one another.

I would have to spend the night under the dugout, I realized dimly. I knew that I should shake off the foggy feeling I had and *think*, but I couldn't. Over and over again, I heard the shot and, over and over again, I saw Mr. Strawbridge fall, shaking his head, no, no, no. Mr. Strawbridge was dead. It didn't seem real. But at that very moment, his body was lying by the bank of the creek.

That thought brought me to my senses. Slowly, an inch at a time, I turned over, lifted my head, and shifted around to where I could see out from under the dugout.

The men had set up a camp of sorts. Two were standing by the fire, stirring something in a pot. The smell drifted over to my hiding place, making my stomach rumble. A few of the others were going through the packs that belonged to Mr. Strawbridge and me.

One of them was standing by the bank of the creek. He was pacing back and forth, holding a lantern, looking down the creek as if expecting someone.

With a sick feeling in my stomach, I saw that Mr. Strawbridge's body lay, untouched, where it had fallen. The men walked around it as if it were no more than a rotting log.

One of the men who was rummaging through our gear said, "Well, he wasn't no lawman. There's bird skins in here, and plumes, too. Looks like old Fancypants was a regular outlaw."

"More birds for us with him gone," answered one of the others.

"So he wasn't no game warden," said the man who had shot Mr. Strawbridge.

"I tell you, no one's gonna take that job after what happened to Bradley," said another.

"If anyone's fool enough to try it, he better hope he don't run into me," called the man by the creek. "Meantime, what do you suppose is keeping those Alford boys?"

I was up on my elbows now, peering out from under the dugout, straining to hear every word the men said. It sounded as if the Alfords were expected to show up. I remembered that Frank Brewer had been looking to hire the Alfords to work for R. J. Munroe. If the Alfords were part of this bunch, I wouldn't be able to rely on them for help, even if they did show up.

I was on my own.

In the quiet evening, I could hear most of the men's conversation pretty plainly.

"A man can't hardly make a living no more," one man complained. "The damn rookeries are plumb shot out."

"Birds are spooky, too," a voice answered. "Used to be you could practically walk right up to 'em and hit 'em over the head."

"I'd hate to have to turn to gator skinning," said another. "That's dirty work, dirtier than this here."

"Hell, most of the gators are gone, too. Time was a man could find lakes full of 'em. I heard of a man took ten thousand gators from one lake and that was just a few years ago. 'Course it was a dry year, and all them gators was holed up, makin' for easy pickin's."

"Well, lucky for us we heard Fancypants shooting today. He got his birds someplace close to here, that's for sure. We'll find 'em. Ought to be able to finish 'em off in a day, two at the most. Then it's payday, boys."

They were talking about finding the rookery, Tommy's and my secret place! They knew it was nearby. All they had to do was watch the skies to see the birds leaving their nests to feed and returning with food for their young ones. They were going to "finish 'em off" in one day. And it would be my fault.

The man who was standing by the riverbank called, "Well, lookee here. A little taste of payday is coming right now."

A skiff with three men in it pulled up to shore. In the light from the fire, I recognized Luke Alford and his son, Bill. The third man was a Seminole I didn't know, probably hired on as a guide.

Luke's voice was low and growly when he spoke. "Didn't think we was going to meet up with them moonshiners, after all. They're hiding themselves so well these days even their customers can't hardly find 'em, let alone the law."

"Well, Alford, what are you waiting for? Pass some of that stuff around. We're thirsty."

Luke reached into the boat and took out four big jars. Then his son pulled out a large tin container.

"No, Bill, leave that rotgut there. That's for selling to the Injuns. That stuff's got so much Red Devil lye in it, it'll soap right up and wash your insides clean out, right, chief?" Luke turned, grinning at the Seminole, who stood silently outside the circle at the fire. The Indian gave no answer.

I watched as the men passed the jars around, some taking long drinks from the jar, others pouring the whiskey into their cups.

Luke must have noticed Mr. Strawbridge's body just then. "Who's that?" he asked.

"Some Yankee, we figure. Thought as how he might be a lawman, but turns out he was pluming, too. Found a bunch of bird skins and feathers on him."

"Who killed him?"

"I did," said a voice. "Figured why take chances?"

"Right."

"How 'bout a little *kee-ho-me* for the chief?" asked Bill, pouring some of the moonshine into a cup and handing it to the Seminole, who drank it down in one long gulp.

"Better than he's used to," muttered one of the men. "But what the hell, he's found us some birds on this trip, that's for damn sure."

I knew some of the Seminoles drank whiskey, and some had taken to hiring out to plume hunters for money. Some, like Tommy's father, never touched the white man's liquor; others couldn't get enough of it. This

Indian liked his *kee-ho-me,* I could tell that right off. He drank down a couple more cupsful, sank down by the riverbank, and stayed there.

The rest of the men were getting pretty drunk, too, by the looks of it. It put me in mind of the bad days when Pa was drinking all the time. I knew whiskey could make men act crazy mean—even kill folks, as they said Pa had done. So I lay low, listening to their rough talk, and trying to think of a plan.

TEN

After lots more moonshine and loud talk, some arguments, and one near fistfight, the plume hunters dropped off to sleep. Some of them lay right where they were, not bothering to get under a blanket or anything. Two of them tried to put up a tent, but it didn't go up so easy, and they got mad and just crawled underneath the canvas. After a while the camp grew quiet, save for an occasional moan or snort from one of the men.

As the sounds of the men died down, the noises of the Florida night grew louder. The skeeters had found my hiding place a long time ago and were worrying at me something fierce. The creek made its splashy sounds, and creatures of all kinds called to one another in the darkness. Rain was falling again and, even under the old dugout, I was soaked to my skin and shivering.

I considered slipping silently past the men, sliding my canoe down to the water, and disappearing down the creek. But each time I began to move, one of the men would roll or twitch or cry out in his sleep. I couldn't count on their drunkenness to help me get away, I thought. It was likely one of them would hear me moving in the underbrush, shoot first, and ask questions later. I didn't want to think about what they'd do if they caught me trying to get away, especially after what I'd heard that night.

All I could do was try to make it through the night without shivering to death, and hope that when they broke camp in the morning they'd leave me my canoe. Without it, I thought, I'm dead.

I was worn out. One minute I was so scared I thought I'd die from it, and the next, so mad I wanted to jump right out of my skin. I'd seen a man killed before my very eyes for nothing more than asking a question. I'd heard men laughing about it as if killing a man were no more than slapping a skeeter. And I'd heard those men planning on shooting every plume bird in the rookery that they could, a rookery they'd probably have passed right by if it hadn't been for me and my big mouth.

It was too late to save Mr. Strawbridge. If only I could save those birds! But, I asked myself in despair, *how?* I was up against eleven men, all armed, none of them shy about shooting. Even if they left Mr. Strawbridge's gun and the canoe, what could I do to stop them all by myself? I fingered the knife at my side, but the idea of using it, even on men such as these, made me feel sick.

Time crept by. I might have slept a little, I wasn't sure. The whole night seemed like one big nightmare, but the coming of morning didn't make it go away. I watched the men wake up, grouchy and quiet, and hoped that daylight wouldn't reveal some clue to my whereabouts. The smell of their food set my stomach to growling again. They ate quickly and began to pack up their gear.

One of the men kicked at Mr. Strawbridge's body with his boot and called, "What're we gonna do with Fancypants?"

The man who had shot Mr. Strawbridge seemed to be the leader. He answered, "I don't care. Throw him in the brush. Just get the body back from the creek, and let's get going."

Like a turtle pulling into its shell, I tried to make myself invisible under the dugout as the man came toward me, grunting with the effort of dragging Mr. Strawbridge's body. He dumped the body several yards from where I lay, holding my breath.

The man started to walk away, then stopped and turned back. He knelt next to Mr. Strawbridge's body and began poring through his pockets. Then he grinned, looked around to see if any of the others were watching, and pulled a wallet from Mr. Strawbridge's trouser pocket.

"Well, well, what have we here?" he muttered softly as his fingers riffled through the wallet. He gave a low whistle as he counted the money. "Much obliged to you, Fancypants," he said, stuffing the wallet in his own pocket. "Much obliged," he repeated. He laughed, gave Mr. Strawbridge's body a final kick, and walked back to where the others were preparing to leave.

"How about this?" asked another man. I looked up to

see what he was talking about. He was pointing at the canoe, my only hope of escape.

"We'll take it," said the leader. "The more boats we have, the more we can spread out over that rookery. Take the plumes and skins, too. And don't forget the gun."

I hadn't realized until that moment just how much I'd been holding on to the hope of having that canoe. As the men in their boats disappeared down the creek, I gave in to the awful misery I felt. Still curled up under the dugout, I cried until I couldn't cry anymore.

When finally I stopped and tried to get up and out of my hiding place, I found I could hardly move. I couldn't feel my arms and legs to make them do what I wanted. Bit by bit, as I inched my way along the ground, the numbness in my limbs went away, only to be replaced with a feeling like thousands of scorpion bites all over my body. I don't know how long it took before I was able to stand and walk to where the men had made camp. I was careful not to look in the direction of Mr. Strawbridge's body.

I was hungrier than I could ever remember being. Our packs were thrown carelessly about, and in the bottom of one of them I found a bowl, a sack of flour, a tin of lard, and some of the jam Mama had packed. With my fingers I scooped out some lard, put it in the bowl, dumped in some flour, and mixed it with my hands. I wasn't about to make a new fire and cook biscuits. I took a great big handful of the mixture in my mouth, then another and another. I finished off my meal with some jam. Then I drank a couple of bowls full of water from the creek.

I looked through the rest of the packs to see what would be of use to me. The men must have had enough food of their own, because they left all of ours. They left the cooking pots, too, and all Mr. Strawbridge's scientific equipment, measuring tools, notebooks, paints, and the like. Our tents were still there, as were our bedrolls and extra clothes, such as they were. All that was missing, really, were the canoe, the gun, the ammunition, and the bird skins and plumes.

And the money.

I could live for a couple weeks on the food. I'd be warm at night, and dry. I could survive without a gun. But in this country, without a boat, I was stuck right where I was. Pa and Mama and Carrie didn't even expect me back for at least a week and a half, and even if they knew I was in trouble, how would they know where to find me? I was on a no-name backwater creek off the main river, where nobody was likely to happen by. The only reason the plume hunters had come this way was 'cause of hearing Mr. Strawbridge's shooting. It could be a long, long time before anyone else came to this particular place.

As the truth of my situation came down on me, I felt like crying again. No, I told myself. No more of that.

What was it Pa had said to me when I left? "You've got a good head on your shoulders, son. If you get into trouble, use it." He'd been smiling when he'd said it, never thinking it might matter. But now it was all I had to hang on to.

Trouble was, my head didn't seem to be working right. The body of Mr. Strawbridge, tossed over in the brush, was beginning to give me the heebie-jeebies. I'd never been up close to a dead body before, much less stranded on an island with one. I began to think of all the old tales I'd heard of ghosts and spirits returning from the dead to take their revenge. I hadn't murdered Mr. Strawbridge, but how could I be sure his ghost would know that?

Ghosts and spirits . . . don't get stupid now, I told myself. Do one thing at a time. The main thing is to get off this island and stop those men.

But first I knew I had to bury Mr. Strawbridge's body. Not, I told myself, because his ghost would haunt me if I didn't, but because it was the right thing to do. I hadn't sorted out yet just what kind of man Mr. Strawbridge had been. He was peculiar, all right, but that didn't mean he deserved to die the way he did and then get left for the varmints.

I found some soft, boggy ground and used my dinner bowl to scoop out enough earth to make a shallow grave. I began to cry again when I walked over to Mr. Strawbridge's body and saw the look of surprise on his face and the little round hole in his chest, clotted with darkened blood.

I dragged him over to the clearing in the ground. For a small man, he was awful heavy. Then, panting from the effort of it, my chest still heaving with sobs, I rolled him into the hole and covered him up.

It didn't seem fitting as a burial for a man, so I tried to think of some proper words to say. "Lord, take this man,

Hugo Strawbridge, into Heaven. He was shot down by some bad men. May he rest in peace. Amen." It was the best I could do.

Then all I wanted to do was get away from there. Hopelessly I looked around for a means of escape. My eyes swept past the dugout that had saved my life the night before, then stopped. The dugout. I ran over and turned it right side up. One end of it was burned right off, but what was left looked to be solid. I tried to think of how I could fix it up to make it seaworthy.

Dragging the old Indian canoe over to the water, I had the idea that maybe I wouldn't have to do much fixing at all. Being made of wood, it would float. Maybe if I stood in the unburned end, I could manage. But damn! My pole was gone, too. I'd have to find a tall, skinny tree to cut for a pole.

I was searching for a suitable tree when I heard shooting. Coming from the direction of the rookery, it was muffled and far away, but there was no mistaking what it was. It sounded like a hundred guns all firing at once, over and over and over again. I thought it would never stop.

Eleven men with guns, expert shooters, spread out on all sides of those nesting grounds. How many birds could they kill? I didn't want to think about it.

Feeling sick, I tried to guess what they'd do next. Even with all the birds scared off, the men would stay put. Those grown-up birds wouldn't know any better than to come right on back, heeding the cries of their young or feeling the pull of the eggs they'd left behind in their nests. And when they did, the hunters would be waiting.

It was a game that would go on until there were no birds left to play.

Furiously I ran from place to place, looking for something, anything I could use to fashion a pole. I needed a tree trunk or branch about twice a man's height, thin so I could hold on to it, light so I could manage it, but strong. Finally I found a spindly cypress. Using my knife, I cut around in a circle, carving out chunks until I was able to push on the trunk above the weakened spot and knock the tree over. I cut off the smaller branches and examined my work. Too thick, too short—but it would have to do.

I returned to the dugout, climbed into the unburned end, and tried poling across the creek. If I balanced myself perfectly, the burned-off end stayed out of the water enough so that I could move along, but every time my weight shifted a little bit, a wave of water came sloshing into the boat.

It would be all right, I thought, if I didn't have far to go. But I did. And I didn't mind being wet, but I had supplies, too. It would be foolish to leave them behind. My life might depend on having food and a dry place to sleep.

I emptied the packs onto the ground. There was the sack of flour, the lard and jam, rice, coffee, sugar, and tinned milk, several pots and pans of different sizes and one more bowl, fishhooks and line, Mr. Strawbridge's scientific equipment, tools, notebooks and paints, and the tents and blankets and lantern. I took one of the tents and wrapped it around and around the burned-off end of the dugout, tied it fast with some fishing line, and dragged the boat back to the water. The canvas worked pretty well to keep the water out. It leaked some, but with both ends closed up, the whole thing handled much more like a boat.

I wanted to travel light, so I left behind some of the pots and most of Mr. Strawbridge's gear. I couldn't leave the paints and notebooks, though, couldn't leave behind all that clean white paper no one had written or drawn on yet. I wrapped everything as carefully as I could in the packs, and then wrapped them again inside the other canvas tent.

My preparations had taken a long time. It was already late afternoon when I pushed the boat away from the island. I knew where I was headed, but not what I was going to do when I got there.

At that moment the silence was shattered once again by the sound of distant guns.

I kept hearing scattered shots as I poled my way nearer to the rookery. Right around sunset, when I was getting close, there was a long burst of shooting. Grimly I imagined the scared-off birds hearing the urgent cries of their young and coming back to their nests for the night, only to be met by the waiting gunners.

In the gathering darkness, I drew as close to the nesting ground as I dared. I could see the outline of two men standing in a canoe, and I watched as they each took a few more shots at the returning birds. I flinched with each explosion, almost as if the lead were hitting my own chest instead of those soft, feathered breasts.

It was awful watching from the dugout, doing nothing. I could feel my hands clenched on the pole, and my jaw clamped shut so tightly I thought my teeth might break apart. Was this how it felt to be really mad—so mad you might kill a man?

But even as I imagined it, I knew that just as I hadn't slit their throats with my knife while they slept, I wouldn't kill those men now even if I had a gun. The rage I felt was at myself as much as at the hunters. Killing them wouldn't make it go away. I didn't know what would.

I camped well away from the plumers that night. But it wasn't far enough to keep me from hearing the shrill, pathetic peeping of hundreds of baby birds, calling for parents who would never be coming back.

ELEVEN

I awoke to the sound of gunfire and lay miserably on my blanket until it stopped. I kept still, staring at the canvas roof of the tent, trying not to hear, trying not to think. But in my mind, I saw the birds dropping from the sky. I heard the shouts and laughter of the men as they gathered their bounty. I watched as they pulled out the long, showy feathers and threw the bodies back into the water.

I waited until the sounds of the men's voices died away completely, and still I lay on my back in the tent. For a while after the shooting, the world was deathly quiet, but soon, I knew, the hungry chirping of the young birds would begin again.

My heart was racing, but the rest of me felt numb with dread as I poled my dugout to the rookery. What I saw I hope never to see again. But no matter what happens, no matter how hard I try, I won't be able to forget it, not ever. For the rest of my life, I'll see that broken-up nesting ground in my mind, and I'll be sick with the sight of it.

The carcasses of the dead birds, stripped of their fancy feathers, were heaped in piles and floating everywhere.

In death they were different, so different from the way they had been in life that it was difficult to believe they were the same creatures. Could these broken, twisted, heavy bodies ever have flown gracefully from treetop to treetop or danced a courting dance, their beautiful feathers bobbing in invitation?

The naked, scrawny heads of the babies poked over the sides of the nests, their mouths open wide for food and water that would never come. I shuddered, looking at them, knowing that their pitiful cries would attract not their parents, who lay dead in the swamp, but hungry predators: raccoons, rats, possums, crows, ants. . . . I looked up and saw the first buzzard, circling eagerly overhead. Soon there would be hundreds. They'd stuff themselves until they were too full to fly.

I made myself stand there and take it all in. I stayed as the buzzards came flopping in and began ripping at the bodies. I stayed as the sky darkened and the night varmints came creeping stealthily in for their share of the kill. I stayed and listened to the crunching, the ripping, the cracking, and the crying until I was too weary and heartsick to stand.

Then I poled back up the river to an island of black mangroves and rolled up in the canvas of my tent on the ground, not caring that I was hungry and wet, not caring that the skeeters were landing on my face and buzzing in my ears, not feeling anything at all. . . .

I slept, and the sounds and sights and smells of slaughter filled my dreams.

When I awoke, the sun was beating fiercely against my

eyelids. I hadn't seen sunshine for a couple days, and at first the sight of it made my spirits lift. But then I remembered.

I wasn't hungry, but I forced myself to make some corn cakes and eat them. I thought vaguely that I should be doing something. Like going home. . . . Like telling someone about Mr. Strawbridge's murder. . . . But instead I was drawn to the rookery once again.

The sun beat down mercilessly on those poor, scraggly young birds. The hot air began to fill with the stink of the rotting bodies of their parents. It was almost a relief to know that the babies would not live through the day.

At that moment two adult great white herons came flying in to find their nests. They had escaped the guns. Now they could tend their young ones, and the young would live and grow to have babies of their own. My eyes flooded with tears at the sight of them, I felt so grateful and happy. It seemed like a miracle. I'd never been much for praying without Mama telling me to, but I closed my eyes right then and there and thanked God for those two birds. Maybe there would be others who would return, I thought hopefully. Not many, I knew, but maybe some.

With the thought of the two live herons as my only consolation, I began poling the dugout in the direction of home. A movement in the mangrove scrub caught my eye. I looked again and saw the outline of a canoe and a strip of brightly colored calico from a Seminole shirt. Then two dark eyes peered at me from among the leafy branches.

"Tommy!" I cried.

The canoe slid quickly through the tangle of mangroves, moving silently away from me.

"Tommy!" I cried again. "Wait! Please, wait!"

Tommy kept poling swiftly away.

Desperately I called again, "Wait! *Thok-fee!*" It was the Miccosukee word for "brother." Tommy had taught me the word, pointing first to me and then to himself. Brothers.

The rookery had been filled with the sounds of life the last time Tommy and I visited it together. Now my cry echoed through the eerie silence. The canoe stopped. Tommy turned. His dark eyes stared into mine, but I could read no expression there.

"No *thok-fee,*" he said.

And then he was gone.

I didn't try to catch up to Tommy. Even if I could speak his language better, what words would I say? I had broken my promise, and now the rookery was shot out. It didn't matter that I hadn't pulled the trigger. I wasn't Tommy's brother. No *thok-fee*. I was *yat-hot-kee,* a white man. Not to be trusted.

Slowly I began poling my way downriver. When I was about a mile or so from home, I came around the end of a small key and came upon Bean, fishing for brim. Most days just seeing Bean's gap-toothed grin was enough to start me smiling, but even his hollered greeting, "Hey, River Rat!" didn't cheer me up right then.

We drew up alongside each other. Bean said, "Why, Tyler, you look like you've been shot, skinned, and set out to dry. Who plucked your plumes, boy?"

I usually liked Bean's colorful way of speaking, but that day his words stung. I didn't answer, not knowing where to begin. Bean gave me a long look. His eyes took in the burned dugout with the tent wrapped around the end, the packs thrown carelessly in the bottom, and then returned to my face.

"Let's pull on up to that high ground over there," he said, pointing to the other side of the river, "and you can tell me what's happened."

When we were seated side by side on the riverbank, Bean said, "You're awful quiet today, Ty. Have you gone Injun on me? Where's Mr. Strawbridge?"

I tried to answer, but my voice got stuck behind the hot tears that were suddenly running from my eyes. Bean didn't act as if this was anything strange. He just made himself comfortable and waited, watching the river flow by. Finally, slowly, I began to tell him some of what had happened. I'd never found it so hard to talk. Every word seemed to take more strength than I had, and at last I stopped.

When I had finished, we sat quietly. Bean seemed to be thinking it all over, in no hurry to speak. At last he said, "It's a terrible thing, watching a man get killed."

I nodded.

"And a shot-out rookery is a hellish sight, Tyler, I know. It's not something a person's likely to forget."

I shuddered, and Bean was quiet for a while. Then he said, "You know, Ty, if it hadn't been Luke Alford and his boy and those other men working for R. J. Munroe, it would have been somebody else who shot up that rookery. It was only a matter of time."

"They'd never have found it if it wasn't for me!" I cried.

Bean shook his head. "As long as those birds have a price on their heads, there'll be somebody comin' round to collect it. They'll find 'em and shoot 'em till there aren't any left to shoot."

"Mr. Strawbridge said something like that," I answered. "He said if he didn't shoot those birds, somebody else would, so it might as well be him who got the money. But he made it sound like when he did it, it was all right because it was *scientific*. He said when the birds were all gone, people would still be able to see them in museums because of him, and that someday his name would be more famous than that Audubon. He was forever calling the birds 'magnificent creatures' and all such as that, but he was shooting 'em like crazy, same as the plumers."

Bean took his time again. Then he said, "Some people are greedy for money. And some are greedy for glory, like that Mr. Strawbridge. But it's all the same, really. To some folks, it doesn't matter what they do to get what they want. And they'll think up the damndest reasons why it's the right thing to do, too."

I thought about what Bean had said. He was right. Just look at the way Mr. Strawbridge had convinced me to show him the rookery. And, I thought uncomfortably, how easily I had convinced myself he was right. And why? For money. For three dollars a day, twenty-one dollars a week, forty-two dollars in the end. For Mama, so she could buy a few things to make her life easier. For Pa, so he wouldn't feel so bad about bringing Mama to a place she hated, and so they wouldn't argue at night. For Carrie, so she could have a dress that fit and something special of her own. Were those good reasons?

The memory of the ruined rookery filled my mind. No. No reasons were good enough for that.

"It's funny, Tyler," Bean went on, talking slowly, as if he was figuring as he spoke. "No, I reckon that's the wrong word. It's *peculiar*, is what it is, but I've been thinking maybe there's places where folks just got no business being. Take this place here, Lostman's River. Most folks only see the skeeters and the heat and all they know is they don't like 'em. They see the birds and the gators and all they think about is how much they can get for 'em. They don't see how everything here has its place, how it fits, even the skeeters. They want to change the place, make it so it suits *them*. Me, I fit here. The Injuns, they've learned to fit here, too, long as nobody bothers 'em. Those birds fit, too, have for a long time." He was quiet for a moment. Then he added, "I don't believe I'd care to live someplace where there was no birds."

"Mr. Strawbridge said that even if the birds aren't all shot off, soon there won't be anywhere left for them to live. He said folks want to move here, but they want to 'civilize' it first. So the governor's digging canals to let all the water run out so folks can build cities and such, and soon there won't be any wet places left for the birds and gators and skeeters."

"I've seen the dredges," said Bean. "You reckon Strawbridge was right?"

I shook my head. "I don't know," I said. "It doesn't seem possible—not looking around here right now." The image of the rookery filled my mind. How fast things could change! "But I guess maybe it *could* happen. If nobody stops it."

"Guy Bradley," said Bean. "He tried to stop the shooting."

And look where it got him, I thought sickly. But Bean was right. At least Guy Bradley had tried. Mr. Strawbridge had already given up.

"Don't know how to go about stopping those dredges," Bean mused.

Right then I felt tired, more tired than I'd ever been in my life.

"You look about done in," Bean said. "Why don't you leave that sorry-looking canoe of yours and let me take you home."

Home. Suddenly I longed to see Mama and Pa and Carrie.

Bean's familiar crooked grin split his face. He wiggled his eyebrows at me and added, "If I'm not mistaken, it's just about time for your Mama to be fixing up some supper."

TWELVE

When Bean and I rounded the river bend that brought our house into view, tears flooded my eyes again. I brushed them away quickly so I could watch Mama, who was coming out the door just then. I saw her shade her eyes, trying to figure who was coming. I waved. Mama kept on peering hard in our direction. Then, recognizing us, she threw up her hands and ran back to the house, and I knew she was calling Pa and Carrie.

They were all three waiting at the landing when Bean and I pulled up. Mama and Pa's faces were full of questions, but Carrie was just plain happy I was home.

"You're back!" she squealed, jumping up on me like a little monkey. She pretty near knocked me over, then she hugged me so hard around the neck I thought I'd choke, but I didn't mind, it felt so good to see her. She drew her head back and looked me in the face. "Where's that man? The one who talked funny."

I hugged Carrie back and set her down on the ground. She looked up at me, waiting for an answer. Mama and Pa, too, were watching my face.

"Ty?" Mama asked anxiously.

I swallowed. I didn't want to tell it in front of Carrie, but they were all waiting for me to say something.

"He's dead," I answered.

Carrie's mouth turned into a big round O, and she wrapped her arms around Pa's legs. Mama's hand flew to her cheek, and her mouth, too, fell open.

"He was—murdered," I went on. "By a man—he was with Luke and Bill Alford—and they were plume hunting, and all he did was ask them did they see any birds, and all of a sudden he was dead, and I was hiding and I watched it happen and—"

It was coming out all mixed-up, but I couldn't help it. Seeing the faces of Mama and Pa and Carrie made me realize how alone I'd felt for the past three days. Now that I was safe at home, all the horror and fear I'd been trying to hold back came rushing over me, and I was crying again, the way I hadn't cried since I was Carrie's age. Pa stepped up and held me in his arms until I could stop my shaking.

Then we all walked into the house together. We sat at the table and Mama served supper, but Bean was the only one who ate much of anything. There was none of the joking and fooling that was usual when Bean was around. Everyone sat, quiet and serious-looking, while I slowly told the whole story. My voice came out kind of wobbly and jerky at first, but even Carrie sat very still, listening.

I didn't know why, but it felt good to tell what had happened. After I'd told about the murder, I told how

Mr. Strawbridge had asked me to show him the rookery, and how I'd done it. How, because of me, Strawbridge had killed some of the birds and the hunters had killed the rest.

It was a relief to tell the shame of it right out loud. When I had finished, everyone was quiet for a long time.

I broke the silence with a bitter laugh. "All that big talk about three dollars a day, and I don't have a penny to show for it." I was glad, too; I didn't want any blood money.

"I expect you'll be going to Key West to pay a visit to the sheriff," said Bean, "there being a murder and all."

Bean didn't know anything about Pa's trouble with the law. He was busy wiping gravy from his chin with his sleeve, a habit I knew drove Mama to distraction. But she didn't even seem to notice. It was Bean's words she was paying attention to, and they had made her face go white.

"The sheriff . . . ?" she repeated. "But . . . we . . ." She stopped, looking at Pa. Their eyes locked. Something passed between them during that long look.

Then Pa turned to Bean. "I expect you're right," he said. "Tyler'll have to tell the sheriff what he saw. We'll leave first thing tomorrow."

To me, he said, "We'll carry that charcoal along with us. It'll take some time to load it up."

I nodded, but I wasn't thinking about the charcoal. I was thinking about Pa going to Key West to see the sheriff, maybe being arrested and taken away to jail!

I felt as if I were in a dream. Bean thanked Mama for dinner and swung Carrie up over his head till she squealed for mercy. Then he told me to come on out with him to the boat to get my things. I followed him in a daze. As I unloaded the packs, full of my own troubled thoughts, Bean was talking.

"Anyone can make a mistake, you know, Ty, the way you did when you showed the rookery to Strawbridge. A smart person looks hard at the situation and learns something from it." He handed me the last of my gear and said, "And, Tyler, you're no fool. You've whupped me at cards enough times so I know that. All right, so you didn't play your last hand so good. Tomorrow you get a new deal, and a chance to make up for that bad hand. The question is: How will you play it next time?"

What was Bean doing, talking about cards? I knew he was trying to make me feel better, but all I could think about was Pa going to jail. I shrugged. "I don't know, Bean," I said.

Bean pushed the canoe away from shore with his pole. "You'll figure it out," he said, and quickly disappeared down the river into the dusky night.

I called good-bye and turned back to the house. When I walked in the door, the house was quiet. Carrie was already in bed, and Pa and Mama were sitting at the table.

I said right out, "What are you talking about, going to see the sheriff? Pa, you know what could happen!"

"Yes, Tyler, I do. But your mama and I believe it's what

we ought to do. You've got to tell someone about what you saw."

"Why?" I demanded. "Why should we bring ourselves—bring you—to the sheriff's attention? We haven't done anything wrong. It's not like I killed Mr. Strawbridge."

"That's just the point, son," said Pa. "You have nothing to hide, but you do have a story to tell. And if you don't tell it, those murderers will get away with what they did."

Had Pa gone simple? Had he forgotten about why we ran from New York in the first place? "But, Pa, you—you *do* have something to hide!"

Pa sighed. "I didn't kill anybody, either, Ty. And it's coming clear to me that I'm tired of acting as if I did."

"Tyler," said Mama, "sooner or later Mr. Strawbridge is going to be missed, and somebody somewhere is going to want to know what happened to him, an important man like he was. There's any number of people who know he came here. Sooner or later you'll have to tell someone what you saw. Which means that sooner or later we'll be dealing with the law, anyway."

"We could just run again," I said. "Someplace no one can find us." Even as I said it, I knew it wasn't any good.

Mama shook her head.

"No," said Pa. "No more running. I'm tired of living on the wrong side of the law, and dragging you all along with me. Running was a bad idea. I couldn't see it then, but I can see it now."

"But, Pa," I said again, still not able to accept what I was hearing, "the law makes mistakes! What about the story Bean told, about how that murderer Smith got off free? How do you know they won't make a mistake and put you in jail, after all?"

"It's a chance we've decided to take, Ty," said Mama. "It's the right thing to do, you'll see."

I stood for a moment, staring hard at Pa's eyes, then at Mama's. I could see they had made up their minds. It didn't matter what I said.

"Go on to bed now, son," said Pa. "You've been through a lot, and we have a big day ahead of us tomorrow."

I turned to go to my room. Why did parents always seem to think that a good night's rest would solve everything? How could I sleep? And how would things be any better in the morning?

Carrie was half asleep when I crawled into my bed. "Ty?" she called sleepily. "Can I come in with you?"

I knew she was expecting me to say no, the way I usually did. But instead I found myself saying yes. "If you promise not to wiggle all night," I warned.

Carrie climbed in next to me and snuggled at my side with a happy sigh.

"And no snoring."

She giggled. Soon I could tell from her soft, regular breathing that she was asleep. It was hours before I, too, slept, but it felt good to have her there beside me.

Thirteen

In the morning Pa shook me awake early, before it was even light out, and I went with him to load the charcoal onto the raft. His eyes were red rimmed and tired looking. I could tell he wasn't much in the mood for talking, so I kept my mouth shut and worked. When we had finished, I went inside to wash up, eat, and get ready to go.

I was surprised to find several large bundles, carefully tied up, sitting by the door, and as I gazed around the room I saw that it looked different. Things were missing: Mama's good dishes were no longer stacked on the sideboard, and the cloth was off the table, along with the silver candlesticks we had brought from New York. I went into the room I shared with Carrie and found Mama folding our clothes and putting them into a pack. The blankets were not on the beds.

"What are you doing?" I asked.

She turned to me, and I saw that her eyes looked tired. She and Pa must have been up half the night, too.

"We're just going to Key West, Mama," I said. "We'll probably be gone three or four days. What do we need with all that stuff?"

"We have to be prepared, Ty," she said, "for—" Carrie walked into the room, and Mama said only, "for whatever happens." Her voice sounded quiet and flat, the way it had in the days before Mr. Strawbridge showed up.

I wanted to ask Mama more, but I figured she didn't want to say too much in front of Carrie. And, in a way, I was afraid to hear the answers. Carrie felt the strangeness, anyway, I could tell. She was sitting silently by the door, hugging her knees, where ordinarily she'd have been dancing around with excitement at the thought of going on a trip down the river.

I went to the hiding place under my bed where I kept all the wooden figures I'd carved. There were the pieces for the crèche I was making for Mama, and others, too. I put the figures, along with my drawings and the art supplies Mr. Strawbridge had brought with him, into one of the bundles and carried it out to the raft. I tried not to think, even to myself, about why I was doing this. The thought that we would never come back here to Lostman's River kept trying to push itself into my mind. I didn't want to think about it. I didn't want to think at all.

I took out two of the figures. One was an egret. I was very proud of it: I'd spent hours carving the delicate feathers in the bird's crest so that each one stood out, separate and distinct. The other was a heron, its long neck folded into a curving shape like an S. I was proud of that one, too; it had been hard to get the long, skinny neck just right.

I wrapped each of the carvings in a piece of canvas.

One I set down in the cleared-off place under the palmetto tree where Tommy and I had sat so many times to work on our carvings. The other I left on the supper table, surely Bean's most favorite place.

Mama was standing down by the river, holding Carrie's hand and waiting silently for Pa to show her how he was planning to arrange us all. The raft was loaded down with the charcoal and the bundles holding our belongings. Pa meant to ride the raft, guiding it with his pole. Mama, Carrie, and I would lead the way in the large canoe, with me poling.

Our goal was to get downriver and up the coast to Storter's trading post in the town of Everglade by that evening. Then we'd catch the first trade ship he had that was going across the Gulf of Mexico to Key West. Ordinarily Pa and I would trade with Mr. Storter for the charcoal, stock up on supplies, and head on up the river to home, making the whole trip in two or maybe three long days. We'd never been to Key West before, and I'd always dreamed of going someday, imagining the trip as a carefree, exciting adventure. But instead of excitement, all I could feel was a sense of dread about what was to come.

We got ourselves settled. Pa checked once more to make sure the load on the raft was fastened tight, and we were off.

As we journeyed down the river, I found myself wishing that we were just a normal family making a trip to the trading post. I began to play games in my mind, seeing that family arriving at the store and carefully selecting their supplies. I pictured the parents telling the children that there was enough money left over for each of them to pick out something special. The girl wanted a pocketknife like her brother's, but her parents laughed kindheartedly and said she had to wait until she was older. The boy looked eagerly at the well-stocked shelves, searching for just the right thing. . . .

But there my imagination failed me. We weren't an ordinary family and hadn't been, really, for a long time. And I didn't feel like a boy any longer. Right then I couldn't think of anything I wanted, nothing I could buy at a store, anyway. It gave me a funny feeling in my stomach, as if I'd lost something, though I couldn't have said what it was.

I looked at my family. Mama sat, staring blindly ahead. I didn't know what she saw inside her head, but I knew she wasn't seeing the river, or the mangroves, or even Carrie and me and Pa.

Carrie, too, sat without saying a word, her face looking awfully serious for a five-year-old girl's. I wished I could cheer her up some way, but that morning I just didn't have it in me to tease her or make a joke.

Pa followed on the raft, concentrating on his poling and keeping quiet. We were all together, but somehow each one of us was alone.

I saw a "slide," the place where a crocodile had climbed up out of the water. Then I saw several of the big reptiles sunning themselves on the banks of the little creeks that fed the river. That meant we were approaching the place where Lostman's River met the sea. Crocs liked the salty water, while gators liked it fresh. But when it came to their hides, crocs were prized the same as gators. I loved seeing their long, greenish gray bodies and sleepy-looking eyes, but I wished they'd learned to be a little more scared of humans. They sure would have been easy to shoot if we'd had a mind to.

Finally we came to where Lostman's River emptied into the Gulf of Mexico. There, at the river's mouth, the fresh water met the salty water, and sometimes it created a current that made navigating tricky. Pa and I had done this lots of times before, and we were extra careful to keep our crafts pointed into the waves. Then we began to head north along the shoreline to Storter's place. We had to work a lot harder without the river's current to help us.

Now that we were off the river, I switched to oars and began to row. Pa tied the raft to our canoe, and he began to row, too. Using strong, even strokes, I was glad to find that I could easily keep up with Pa's rhythm. Of course the canoe was easier to manage than Pa's big, square raft, but, still, I had the weight of three people, and I couldn't help feeling proud as we moved swiftly along the shoreline.

The wind was from the south, and that was a big help. It pushed us up the coast and kept us close to land. If we'd had a north wind, we'd probably have had to wait for another day. As it was, I knew we were making good time and would reach George Storter's store that night, sometime after sunset.

The air was warm, and the salt in it smelled fine and tasted good on my lips. I saw several tarpon rolling in the shallows. When we spooked them, they went swimming past like silvery, underwater ghosts. A school of porpoises came and swam along beside us, and for a few moments I was able to forget everything but the thrill of watching their sleek, shining bodies flying easily through the water. But then the uncertainty of what would happen when we got to Key West returned.

When we pulled up to the boat landing at Storter's, the sun had already sunk into the sea, and a drizzly rain was falling. Usually I was glad to see Mr. Storter and interested to hear all the news. But that night I was relieved that the gathering darkness hid our faces as Mr. Storter helped us tie up at the boat landing. He showed us where we could camp for the night and said, "You're in luck, folks. I've got a boat leaving for Key West in the morning. First thing tomorrow I'll take a look at that charcoal of yours, Will, and we'll make us a deal." He peered at us curiously and seemed about to ask a question. But all he said was, "Y'all look done in, so I'll leave you be now. We'll be sailing early."

We set up our tent and ate a quiet supper. Then we went to bed. As Carrie curled up next to me, I was grateful that the hard work of poling and rowing all day meant that I'd sleep. I didn't think I could stand another night full of my own gloomy thoughts chasing themselves around inside my head, going nowhere.

126

FOURTEEN

Mr. Storter woke us in the morning and told Pa he'd pay thirteen dollars for the charcoal. He said that since he was going to Key West, anyway, there'd be no charge for the four of us to come along. I thought that was mighty generous of the captain, and Pa did, too.

The sun was just coming up as we set sail in the trading sloop, the *Bonito*. Carrie and I stood on the deck, watching the sunrise. Luck seemed to be with us again; the wind had changed to a steady westerly blow, and whitecaps licked the surface of the sea as we headed south down the coast.

Standing on the deck with Carrie, I wished for time to stop so we could stay right where we were, with the troubles we'd had at Lostman's River behind us and the ones that waited for us in Key West never to come. The feeling was so strong that I actually held my arms out, palms facing away from me, as if I could hold back the passing of the minutes that way. I swear that if I could have, I'd have stood right there forever, with Carrie next to me, the wind in my face and the sun shining brightly on the wide sea all around.

But then Mr. Storter walked over to where Carrie and I stood. "Your mother tells me you do some wood carving, Ty," he said.

"Yes, sir," I answered. "Animals and birds, mostly."

"Would you let me take a look at them?" he asked.

Surprised, I said, "Sure. I'll go get them."

I ran to the cabin and brought back the pack that held my wooden figures. One by one I removed them and handed them to Mr. Storter.

"Mmm. Very good, Ty, very good," he said, turning over each figure in his hands and examining it. "There's a fellow by the name of Brock in Key West who has been buying wooden figures to sell. Seems Yankees'll spend good money for 'em. Gators and crocs are popular, along with the plume birds. Flamingos are big sellers, too. Those Audubon fellers and other bird lovers buy 'em, I guess. Your mother tells me you do drawings, too."

"Yes, sir," I said, and handed him a sheaf of papers from the pack.

"These look quite good to me, Tyler. Of course, I'm no expert, but you've certainly captured the likeness of these birds. Are you interested in selling any of these?"

It was strange to think that anyone would pay money for something I liked to do just to pass the time. I remembered how Mr. Strawbridge had said I had talent when it came to such things. Well, I thought, we could always use the money.

"The crèche figures are for Mama," I said. "But when I finish hers, I can make more. And I can carve or draw any kind of bird or animal you want, sir."

"I'll go to see Mr. Brock when we get to Key West," said Mr. Storter. "I'll see how he likes your work and what kinds of things he thinks will sell. How does that sound?"

"Good, Mr. Storter. Thank you," I said.

Mr. Storter walked away and I looked at Carrie and smiled. "Maybe I'll be able to buy you something special, after all," I said.

Pa had said it was about one hundred miles from Storter's to Key West, and that the trip would take anywhere from one and a half to two days, depending on wind and weather. As it was, we made pretty good time, arriving at the dock on Key West late the next morning.

When we were leaving the ship, Mr. Storter stopped us. "I'll be sailing back first thing tomorrow," he said. "You're welcome to come along. Will, I'll let you know what that skinflint Mercer has to say about the market for charcoal, see if it's worth your time making some more. And, Tyler, I'll find out what kind of a deal I can make with Brock."

Pa nodded, and Mama and I murmured our thanks. We stood uncertainly in the glare of the hot, sunny streets, not sure what to do or where to go.

"Which way to the sheriff's office?" Pa asked quietly.

Mr. Storter gave a snort. "You'd be lucky to find Sweeney in his office," he said. "You'll have better luck at the tavern at the end of the street here." He pointed to his left. "The Blue Dolphin. Look for a skinny, weasely looking fellow sliding off his bar stool. That'll be our fine sheriff," Mr. Storter finished with a lift of his eyebrow and a funny twist to his mouth. He waited, hoping, probably, for some inkling as to what our business was with Sheriff Sweeney.

But all Pa said was, "Obliged," and we headed off in the direction Mr. Storter had shown us.

As we walked down the street, I held on to Carrie's hand. She was gazing about her with amazement, and I realized that she had never in her short life been anywhere farther than Mr. Storter's trading post. And where folks from big cities like New York or Philadelphia might not think Key West was much, Carrie was speechless with wonder.

I had to admit that I, too, was excited by the sights of so many people and so much activity. The area near the docks was bustling with business as people bought, sold, and traded for fruits, vegetables, meat, fish, turtles, and all sorts of other goods that came in on the ships. There was even an electric streetcar! Carrie wanted to ride it, and so did I, but Pa shook his head and Mama said, "Maybe later." After the peace and quiet of Lostman's River, the sounds and smells of Key West were almost too much to take in, especially when my mind was filled with thoughts of coming face-to-face with the sheriff.

We passed a place with a sign that said HOTEL DUVAL. A wide porch led to a cool-looking room where nicely dressed folks were sitting under a ceiling fan, sipping from glasses of iced tea and lemonade. Pa looked at Mama and said, "Why don't you and Carrie wait here and have yourselves a lemonade while Tyler and I try to find this Sweeney fellow."

Mama started to protest, and I knew that she was worrying about what the cost of a drink might be in such a place. But then she nodded, seeing that Pa was right in not wanting Carrie along. Carrie was already racing up the stairs to the porch, and Mama called sharply, "Carolyn Louise, you wait for me and walk like a lady."

I waved good-bye to Carrie and Mama, wishing that I, too, were going inside for a cool drink. Pa and I walked until we saw a sign cut in the crude shape of a dolphin hanging outside a wood frame building. The sign was painted blue, but the paint was faded and peeling, and I could hardly make out the words THE BLUE DOLPHIN.

Pa turned to me. "You ready, son?" he asked.

I shrugged.

We stepped inside the darkness of the Blue Dolphin, and for a few moments I couldn't see anything after the harsh white glare of the street. I smelled smoke from cigars and cigarettes and a sweetish-sour smell I recognized right off from the old days. Whiskey. I heard men's voices and their laughter. I hoped they weren't laughing at us.

When my eyes became accustomed to the darkness, I saw Pa walking up to a dark-haired man who was sitting at the bar. "Sheriff Sweeney?" I heard Pa say.

"Who wants to know?" the man replied without even looking at Pa.

"My name's Will MacCauley," Pa answered. "I'm here to see the sheriff. Is that you?"

The dark-haired man ignored Pa and spoke to the man behind the bar. "Did you hear that, Ed? He wants to see the sheriff. Sounds like o-fficial business." He ran his hand through his hair, brushing back the greasy strands that had fallen in front of his face. "Well, damn." Again he addressed the man behind the bar. "I reckon that the sheriff would be me, would it not?"

The man behind the bar looked at Pa. "You're lucky," he said. "He knows who he is today."

"What is it you want, Mr.— What was it?" the sheriff asked Pa, turning for the first time to look at us.

"MacCauley," said Pa. "Will MacCauley. This here's my son, Tyler. We've got something to report to the sheriff."

"Well, you're looking at him," the man said. "So report."

"Here?" asked Pa.

The sheriff laughed. "This here's my office," he said. "The Blue Dolphin. Home of law and order in Key West."

Pa looked hard at the man on the stool. "There's been a murder."

The sheriff groaned. "Damn and damn again."

Pa frowned.

"What fool went and got himself shot?"

"A man by the name of Hugo Strawbridge," Pa answered. "He was a scientist. Sort of like one of those Audubon folks."

The sheriff held his hands up to his face and groaned again. "Don't talk to me about those Audubons," he said.

"They're all over me already, wanting me to find a replacement for their man Bradley. They actually wanted me to go out there into those swamps that God forgot and get myself shot over a bunch of bird feathers! Not bloody likely, I told 'em. Not bloody likely."

"Look," said Pa. "Do you want to hear about what Tyler saw or not?"

The man looked at me for the first time. The man behind the bar was looking mighty interested, too. "You saw this murder, sonny?" the sheriff asked me. "Where did it take place?"

Before I could answer, he said to the man behind the bar, "If it wasn't in this county, it's outside of my jurisdiction. Not my problem, if you see what I mean." To me he said again, "So where did you say the murder took place? No, wait, wait, don't tell me here. What say we go down the street to my office and get this down real official-like. Isn't that what you wanted in the first place?"

The man slid down off the bar stool and reached up as if he meant to straighten his tie, only he didn't have one on. Pa and I looked at each other, not knowing what to make of this Sheriff Sweeney. We went with him out of the Blue Dolphin and turned to the right. The glare of the sun made all of us squint, but somehow I had the feeling it hurt Mr. Sweeney's eyes worst of all. He muttered to himself all the way to his office, which to my surprise was exactly as I'd pictured a sheriff's office, right near a court-house building with a jail attached to it and everything.

He didn't tell us to sit down, but we did, anyway, and

he sat across from us at his desk. He seemed a little more like a sheriff then, and began acting a little more like one, too. He asked me all about what I had seen and heard. He didn't much like it when I said I didn't know a name for the place where Mr. Strawbridge died, but I could take Mr. Sweeney there if he wanted.

"Sounds like it could have taken place in Collier County," he said hopefully.

I remembered the words carved in the stone of the courthouse building: MONROE COUNTY COURTHOUSE, and figured that if the murder had happened outside of Monroe County, it was outside of what the sheriff called his "jurisdiction." And that meant, I guessed, that he wouldn't have to do anything about it.

I was beginning to think that even if the murder *had* taken place within his jurisdiction, there wouldn't be very much in the way of an investigation by Sheriff Sweeney. He seemed most worried about the Audubon Society "coming down on his back," as he called it, and worried that Mr. Strawbridge might have rich or powerful friends and relatives who would want him to do something. I told him all I knew about Mr. Strawbridge and gave him the card that Mr. Strawbridge had given to me the day he'd stepped onto our landing.

To my surprise, the sheriff didn't want to know anything much about either Pa or me, and there wasn't, as I had feared, a big sign up in his office with a likeness of Pa's face and the word WANTED across the top.

"Where is it you say you live?" Sweeney asked.

"Lostman's River," said Pa.

"Whereabouts exactly would that be?" asked Sweeney.

"About ninety miles up the coast, then a few miles up the river," Pa answered.

"See lots of plumers up that way?" Sweeney asked.

"That's about all we do see," said Pa. "It's lonely country."

"Hmm," said Sweeney, as if he was thinking something over. "You a plumer yourself? Not that you'd tell me if you were."

"No," said Pa. "That kind of work never interested me much. And after what Tyler saw, why, it appeals to me even less."

"Mr. MacCauley, what I'm thinking over here is a business proposition for you. A deal, so to speak."

Pa's eyes narrowed, and I remembered Frank Brewer and his deal, and Hugo Strawbridge and his business proposition. What did Sheriff Sweeney have on his mind?

"I've got a situation here, Mr. MacCauley. You see, those Audubon folks are still in an uproar about Bradley. They want me to find a new warden to replace Bradley, and they want it quick. But nobody in his right mind will touch the job. I don't exactly have a line forming outside my door, if you see my meaning, MacCauley."

Pa didn't answer. He just sat there, waiting to hear what the sheriff would say next.

"Now, you may think a sheriff who had to be rousted from the Blue Dolphin isn't much of a sheriff, and you may be right. But I've got eyes, MacCauley, and I notice things. Take you, for instance, and the boy there. You're not from these parts. I can hear the Yankee in your way of talking. So I ask myself, what's this man MacCauley doing way the hell out on Lostman's River? And I answer myself, I say, he's trying to be a lost man, that's what he's doing."

The sheriff paused to laugh at his joke. I could feel my chest tightening up and my heart beginning to pound. Here it comes, I thought. The man's been playing with Pa, and now's when he'll arrest him.

Pa sat still as could be. He wasn't even looking at Sweeney anymore, but someplace up over Sweeney's head, as if he was thinking about something else. I wondered if his heart was racing the same way mine was.

Sweeney swung his legs up on top of his desk and looked at Pa with a smile that I trusted about as much as a gator's grin.

"On the run, aren't you, MacCauley? Or is that your real name?"

"Name's McLeod," said Pa. "William McLeod."

Oh, no, I thought. I wanted to grab Pa's arm and drag him out of that office and run away before he could say another word. But I sat in my chair like one of my own carved wooden figures.

"What are you running from? Murder, is it?"

"Yes," answered Pa quietly.

"Where'd you run from?"

"New York."

Sweeney whistled under his breath. "You're a long way

from home, Yank," he said. "Did you do it? The murder, that is?"

"No," said Pa, "but I can't remember much about what happened that night. I was drunk. You ought to be able to understand that."

Sweeney chuckled. "Too-shay, McLeod, as they say in France. So you woke up next to a stiff and ran, is that it?"

"Yes," said Pa. "But I don't believe in my heart that I killed him."

Sweeney smiled, shaking his head back and forth. "You don't believe in your heart that you killed him. That's good, McLeod. Just where do you believe it, in your trigger finger?" Again Sweeney laughed heartily at his own little joke.

"I didn't think anyone would believe me," said Pa.

"A wise assumption if that's all you got to say in your own defense," said Sweeney. "How long ago did all this happen, McLeod?" he asked.

"Going on six years," answered Pa.

"I see," said Sweeney. "Well, McLeod, you know what I could do right now, of course, don't you? I could lock you up, send word to New York that I've got their fugitive, and arrange for you to go back there to stand trial. There's no statute of limitations on a capital offense, you know. And murder, why, that's capital with a capital *C*."

I'd never heard the words *statute of limitations* before, but I figured I knew what Sweeney meant. He meant that Pa would always be wanted for murder in New York, no matter how much time went by.

Sweeney was enjoying himself, I could see that, and it

made me want to push the man's legs off his desk and wipe the smile off his face. Didn't he know how Pa and I were feeling right then? Pa's whole life was in Sweeney's hands. But of course Sweeney knew it, and he was making the most of it.

"You've been mighty lucky so far, McLeod," Sweeney went on. "And it could just be that your luck is going to hold. Yessir, coming to see me could be the luckiest thing you ever did. Because you see, I think I can use your help. And you, McLeod, need my help. Very badly."

Sweeney swung his legs to the floor and leaned forward, looking hard at Pa. "I need someone to fill Bradley's shoes to keep those crazy, bird-loving Yanks off my neck. And soon somebody's going to want me to find the killer of that Strawbridge. Most folks couldn't care less, but there's a few who'll raise a hue and cry and want to know what I'm going to do about it. So here's what I'm thinking. What if I suggest that *you* be hired as the new game warden in charge of enforcing the plume laws? That'll get those damn Audubons off my neck. And, as warden, it'll be your job to track down those plumers who did the killing. It'll be you risking your neck out in those skeeter-infested backwaters over a bunch of bird feathers, not me. Say yes, and I'll forget I ever heard about William McLeod. As far as I'm concerned, you'll be William MacCauley, agent of the law. The idea has a certain humorous twist to it, don't you agree?"

I could feel my mouth drop open. I turned to look at Pa, and he looked as stunned as I felt. I could hardly take in the idea of Pa being an accused murderer one minute and being almost like a sheriff or something the next. Say yes, Pa, I wanted to shout! Say yes!

Pa cleared his throat. I waited for him to agree, but instead he said, "I'll need to think it over, Sweeney."

Sheriff Sweeney frowned. "Think it over?"

"I've got a family," said Pa. "I'll be wanting to talk it over with my wife."

"Who is it wears the pants in the family, if I might ask," said Sweeney sarcastically, "you or your wife?"

Pa ignored him. "I'll let you know first thing tomorrow morning."

"I don't see as how you've got a whole lot of choice, but, by all means, 'talk it over.' I don't suppose I have to worry about you running off, now, do I?" added Sweeney with a smirk.

"It was me who came to you in the first place, remember? I'm not running anymore," said Pa. "Where'll I find you? The Blue Dolphin?"

"Watch it, MacCauley," said Sweeney. "Don't get too smart with me. You'll find me right here. And you'd better be here, too. First thing tomorrow."

Pa stood up, so I did, too. We left Sheriff Sweeney sitting in his office, smiling, and walked out into the glare and heat of the street.

FIFTEEN

As Pa and I walked back to the Hotel Duval, I had to know. "You're going to do it, right, Pa?" I asked.

"We'll see, son," was all he said.

When we got to the hotel, Mama and Carrie were gone. At first Pa was worried, but a lady who worked there told us Mama had said they were going out to look around a bit and would be back soon. Pa and I ordered lemonades and sat, waiting.

Soon Mama and Carrie came in. Carrie looked red-faced and hot, and she was rubbing her eyes the way she did when she was tired. She climbed into my lap and leaned against my shoulder.

Mama sat down and looked at Pa. "Well?" she asked.

Pa told her everything Sweeney had said, and about his offer to make Pa into a game warden. She kept shaking her head as if she couldn't believe what she was hearing.

"You mean he knows you're wanted for Davenport's murder," she said, "and he's going to simply ignore it?"

"That's right," said Pa. "Maybe he believed me when I told him I never killed anybody, I don't know. He doesn't really care, not so long as I can solve his problem for him. But, Mary, I've been thinking about it. This way I'd be working for the law instead of running from it. I'd earn a salary. No more running. No more hiding. We could finally put New York behind us."

"You think this would put New York behind us?" Mama asked.

"Yes," said Pa. "I do."

"And we'd go back to Lostman's River?" Mama said.

"That's right," answered Pa.

"And you'd be forever beholden to Sheriff Sweeney to keep your secret."

Pa looked uncomfortable. "I suppose so, yes."

"If you don't do everything just the way he wants, he could turn you in anytime he liked," Mama went on, her voice rising.

"Yes, but the way he sees it, the arrangement is to his advantage, too, Mary."

But Mama just kept talking, her voice getting higher and louder, and in it I could hear the tears she was trying to hold back: "And you'd be off in the swamps chasing after murderers, leaving me and the children behind in that desperate place, wondering if you'd ever come back, wondering if you'd been shot in the back and left for the buzzards?" Usually Mama waited to talk about such things until she thought Carrie and I couldn't hear, but she seemed to have forgotten we were even there.

"It'd be a new start, Mary."

"It doesn't sound new to me," said Mama. "It sounds

141

like more of the same horrible heat, and sun, and skeeters, and even worse danger and fear, and— Oh, what's the use, Will? It's no kind of life for the children. It's no kind of life at all." She stopped, and sat looking down at her lap, her shoulders shaking.

"Mary," Pa said quietly, "the night Davenport was killed has been haunting us for almost six years. I can never get that night back, Mary, or any of the nights I lost to whiskey. I've paid a high price for them. You've paid, too. I know that. But I don't believe I killed Davenport. When I came to my senses and saw him dead, I was sick with the sight of it."

I nodded, remembering the way I'd felt when I saw Mr. Strawbridge lying on the ground, dead.

"I've never for a moment believed you were a murderer, Will," said Mama.

"Then don't you see?" said Pa eagerly. "We came here to report the murders knowing there was a risk of me being arrested. I told myself, if it happens, so be it: At least the running and hiding will be over, and the fear of being caught. But now Sweeney's offering us a whole new chance, Mary. A chance for us to be on the right side of the law, where we belong. It's a chance to make something good out of coming here to Florida." He paused and added, "I don't see as how I have much choice in the matter."

I could hear the pleading in Pa's voice. It made my own throat ache to hear it. I didn't know if Mama understood or not, but I did. Because, like Pa, I'd done something I wasn't proud of, and I needed to find a way to make up for it.

"But you do, Will," said Mama. "You do have a choice."

I watched as Pa reached one of his big red hands out to gently touch Mama's face, as if he wanted to stop her from saying any more. Mama took his hand in one of hers, held it against her face, and sighed. It was one of the saddest sounds I'd ever heard.

"Will, when we left the river to come here, you know I brought my silver candlesticks and the china and everything else I thought I could get money for. This afternoon, while you were talking to Sweeney, I sold it all. I wanted to be ready for—for whatever happened. Well, here's the money, Will," she said, placing a pile of bills on the table. "It's more than enough to get us to New York."

I don't know how long we sat like that: Pa with his hand on Mama's cheek, Mama with her hand holding Pa's, tears sliding silently down her cheeks, Carrie sleeping in my lap, her hair damp with sweat against my chest. It seemed like a very long time.

So many thoughts were going through my mind at the same time, I felt dizzy. New York. I tried to picture it, but all I could remember were buildings and streets and shops. Going back home. But New York wasn't home. Home was Lostman's River.

In my mind I heard Mr. Strawbridge telling me, "Alligators, plume birds, panthers, mosquitoes—they have no place in civilization." I remembered Bean Thompson saying, "I don't believe I'd care to live someplace where there was no birds." How could I live in a place where the only trace of an egret or a flamingo was the feather on a lady's hat, the only sign of an alligator the leather of a purse or a belt or a pair of shoes?

Suddenly I heard my own voice say, "I'm not going."

There was a silence while Pa looked from Mama to me. "Ty," he said finally, "I—"

But I broke in, excited about the idea that was forming in my mind. "I want to stay, Pa," I said. "You'll need help if you're the warden. And, well, Bean Thompson said something to me when he left the other night, and I didn't really understand it till just now. I thought he was just talking about playing cards, but he wasn't. He said I didn't play my last hand very well, but he said every day gives you a new deal."

I knew I wasn't making a whole lot of sense, but I kept on talking, anyway. "Pa, you know what you were saying about—about making some good out of coming to Florida? Well, I was thinking that maybe if I help you to protect the rookeries, it would help make up for what I did."

Mama and Pa both looked at me with puzzled expressions on their faces.

"For all the birds getting shot on account of me," I explained.

"But, Tyler," Mama began.

"Mama," I said, "if Pa's the warden, it'll be his job to protect the birds. And if I help, it'll be, well, you know, like a new hand. And I can play it right this time."

I didn't say out loud the idea that had sprung into the back of my mind. I hardly dared to think it. But maybe, just maybe, if Tommy found out I had the job of protecting the rookeries, he would figure out what had happened and forgive me.

And maybe I'd be able to forgive myself.

"I'm not sure I understand this, Tyler," said Mama. "But the idea of your doing what you're talking about, why, it scares me to death. Think of the danger!"

There was a moment while I thought about what Mama had said. Sure it was dangerous. But didn't that just show how much it needed doing?

"Ty," said Pa, "I know how you're thinking. Because Sweeney's offer sounded mighty good to me, too, at first. But your mama's right. You've got no business chasing down murderers, and neither have I. We'd likely get ourselves killed, and your mama and Carrie would be left alone. And we'd still have to worry about Sweeney turning me in someday, or somebody else figuring out who I was. . . . No, Tyler, I guess I know now what we have to do."

He turned to look at Mama. "We're going back to New York."

SIXTEEN

We spent our last night in Florida at the Hotel Duval. It was funny—no, it was peculiar, as Bean would say—but Mama and Pa were acting happy, almost silly, now that the decision had been made to leave. I couldn't understand it. Mama's voice was full of excitement, the way it had been when she'd talked to Mr. Strawbridge, the way Pa said it used to be before we came to Florida.

She told Carrie that we'd be leaving in the morning on a ship headed north, and Carrie cried. "But, Mama, I don't want to go to New York. I want to go *home*. I want *all* of us to go home."

"But, Carrie, New York *is* home. We've got family there. Right at first, until we get ourselves settled, we'll live with your Aunt Carolyn. Why, you've never even met my sister, your very own aunt, or any of your cousins. And we'll go to concerts and to the park, and Aunt Carolyn has indoor plumbing, and you'll go to school and have friends and nice new dresses."

None of that meant much to Carrie, raised the way she had been, running free in the backwoods. Lostman's River was the only home Carrie had ever known.

"Is there a streetcar in New York?" she asked.

"My, yes," said Mama. "And all sorts of other wonderful things."

"Could we ride *this* streetcar tomorrow?" Carrie asked.

Pa said, "I'll have to go see Sweeney in the morning to tell him what we've decided. While I'm doing that, you all can ride the streetcar. We've got time before the ship leaves."

Carrie's face lit up, and she clapped her hands.

I asked, "Can I go with you to see Sweeney, Pa?"

"I don't see why not," he said.

"Don't you want to ride with us, Ty?" Carrie asked.

"I guess I'll have lots of rides in New York," I said. I was trying to share in Carrie's excitement, but really I was hoping she would go to sleep soon. I needed to ask Mama and Pa some more questions.

Finally, when I was pretty sure she had drifted off, I whispered, "Pa, are you afraid of going to jail?"

Pa was quiet for a while. Then he said gently, "You want to know the truth, Tyler? This is the first time since the night we up and ran that I *don't* feel scared. I feel as though a load has been lifted off my back. I feel—well, I guess it might seem an odd word to use, but I feel free for the first time in close to six years. No, Tyler, I'm not afraid. I'm ready to face whatever comes. I guess if you're not running, you don't have to worry about being caught."

I didn't answer, and he added, "Whatever does happen, Ty, we'll get through it together."

147

I didn't understand how Pa could be so calm. "But what do you think *will* happen?" I asked.

"From now on," Pa answered, "I'm putting my trust in the Lord and in the law, the way I should have done in the first place. That's all I can do, Ty, hope that they'll believe me. For all I know, they may have found Davenport's killer, though I suppose that's unlikely. But I'm thinking that a man turning himself in of his own free will has a better chance of being believed than one who's caught on the run. I'm figuring they'll see I've got nothing on my conscience but the burden of running away."

I tried to smile back at Pa. I could see that somehow he and Mama were feeling a whole lot better than I was about what we were doing, and I wanted to think that Pa was right in trusting in the Lord and the law. And in his innocence, I reminded myself.

I lay thinking about everything Pa and Mama had said. Being on the run had always felt scary; I was glad that part was over. Going to New York and facing up to the law sounded like the right thing to do. But it meant we had to leave what was home to Carrie and me. And while it made Pa feel like he was putting the past behind him, what about me? What could I do now about all those birds getting shot? Bean had said I'd figure it out. But nothing I could think of helped.

Thinking about Bean made a lump come up in my throat. I hadn't even had a chance to say good-bye. I'd known what I was doing, of course, when I'd left the wooden figures, the egret and the heron. I'd left them hoping Bean would find one and Tommy the other, hoping that somehow they'd know all the things I wished that I could say to them now. In my heart I'd known we might not ever go back to our house on Lostman's River. And now it was really happening.

I dreamed that night that I was a mangrove tree. In the dream something was tugging hard at my branches. Whatever it was, it was big, much bigger than I was, and it reached for me and pulled until it had torn my sturdy roots right out of the mud. They dangled in the air, ripped up from where they had buried themselves deep in the ground by Lostman's River. I awoke with a cry, my heart pounding. I was surprised to find the pillow damp and tears running down my cheeks.

SEVENTEEN

Pa and I found Sheriff Sweeney in his office, as he had promised we would. I figured it was too early in the day for him to have had a drink, because he appeared sober. But his voice still had its mocking edge.

"Well, MacCauley? Or should I say, McLeod? Did you and the little woman talk it over?"

"I'm turning myself over to the law in New York," Pa said. He'd always been one for stating things plainly.

Sweeney pushed himself back in his chair, setting his boots up on his desk. He lifted his eyebrows and said, "My, my, my. What, may I ask, made you decide to do a thing like that?"

"I don't think you'd understand," said Pa.

"So I'm supposed to believe you? Just let you walk out of here free as a bird because you tell me you're turning yourself in?"

Pa shrugged. "You can believe it or not. You could hold me, turn me in yourself. But I hope you won't do that. I'd like to do this my way, Sweeney."

"And what exactly is your way?" the sheriff asked.

"To walk in of my own free will and tell my story," said Pa. "And hope they believe me."

"You're just crazy enough to do it, aren't you?" said Sweeney.

Pa didn't answer.

"You think it'll look better for you, doing it that way?" Sweeney asked.

"I thought it might," Pa answered.

"You're probably right," Sweeney said, almost to himself.

"We've booked passage on a ship heading north," said Pa. "It leaves within the hour."

There was a long silence. I thought of all the things Sweeney could do to ruin Pa's plan, and my knuckles turned white from clenching my fists so tight.

The sheriff finally spoke. "What you're doing, McLeod . . . I can't make up my mind about it. Could be that it's real what you might call brave. Then again, it just might be the most foolhardy damn thing I've ever heard of. But what the hell. Either way, I'm not going to stop you. Go on. Catch your ship. Get out of here. I got other things to worry about."

Pa looked startled. "Thank you, Sweeney," he said. "That's real decent of you."

We turned and headed for the door. "Hey, McLeod," Sweeney called after us, "if you ever do talk to the law, don't mention that we met."

Pa said we had one more thing to do. We went to the dock where Mr. Storter was preparing the *Bonito* to sail back up the coast. He raised his eyebrows when Pa and I came on board. "I was wondering if y'all were coming," he said. "Where's the womenfolk?"

"They're not coming," Pa answered. "None of us are. We're going back north, George, where we came from. Came to say good-bye, and to thank you for your kindness."

I could tell Mr. Storter wanted to ask more questions, but all he said was, "Well, is that a fact. We're going to miss you around here, Will. You, too, Tyler. That reminds me," he said, reaching into his pocket. "Here's your charcoal money. Too bad you're leaving. Mercer said he'd buy all I could carry. Tyler, Mr. Brock liked your carvings, and the drawings, too."

"Really, sir?" I asked.

"Said to bring him anything you wanted to sell," said Mr. Storter.

It felt good to think that Mr. Brock, whoever he was, thought my work was good enough to sell in his store. I thanked Mr. Storter again for taking the trouble, and Pa and I said our good-byes.

We walked along the docks, watching the sponge fishermen unloading their smelly catch and listening to them calling back and forth in a language that Pa said he thought was Greek. We heard other languages, too, mostly Spanish, as hundreds of fishermen and businessmen and well-dressed shoppers crowded the dockside markets. The streetcar went by, merrily clanging its bell, and the sharp smell of tobacco from the cigar factories mingled with the smells of fish, fruit, salt water, sweat, and ladies' perfume. We passed shops offering beer, wine, cold drinks, dry goods, coconuts, ice cream, and many other things unfamiliar to me. A banana boat had just docked, and men were unloading the bananas. When they had finished, an auction bell rang, and merchants began to gather to bid on the newly arrived goods. A boy about my age strolled by, selling newspapers. "*Key West Citizen* here. Get yer *Key West Citizen* here," he called.

Maybe I can get a job like that in New York, I thought.

Soon we reached the dock with the ship that would carry us north. Mama and Carrie were waiting. When Carrie saw us, she came running. "Pa! Tyler! You should have come on the streetcar! It went so fast and the bell rang and I waved to all the people. There were so many people! We saw a house—Mama said it was a library, and it's full of nothing but books! And we had ice cream. I tried to save you some, Ty, but it got all drippy so I ate it."

"Sounds like somebody's been enjoying herself," Pa said with a smile.

"She's going to like New York, too," said Mama. "Won't you, Carrie?"

Carrie looked at me. "Mama says you used to live there when you were my age, Ty," she said. "Was it nice, like here in Key West?"

I didn't remember all that much about New York, but I'd been happy enough there, I guessed. New York, as I recalled, was alive the same way Key West was alive. People were everywhere, things were happening. Lostman's

153

River, the only other place Carrie knew, was alive, too, but in a different way. I was trying to think how to explain it to her when the ship's whistle blew three long blasts. It sounded loud and impatient.

"Come on," said Mama, "it's time to board. Everyone carry something."

We stowed our gear in our cabin and began to look around the ship. Carrie was wild with excitement at being on such a big boat. It *was* exciting.

I left Mama and Pa and Carrie and walked to the stern as the whistle gave a final blast and the ship pulled away from the harbor. I watched the docks of Key West grow smaller. Then the ship turned east and began following the long string of keys that would lead us to the tip of Florida.

I watched the mangrove-covered islands slip past. They were so similar to those on Lostman's River, so familiar. I had the drawings I'd made for Mr. Strawbridge, but I knew I'd never forget how the mangroves looked, with their silly red legs walking through the water, or the rich smell of the mud near their roots, or the black crabs that lived there.

I closed my eyes and pretended I was poling my canoe, and I could see the river's beauty and feel its peacefulness. When I opened my eyes, I saw a sea turtle swimming by, a heron feeding in the shallows, and a school of mullet jumping crazily out of the water. My heart was so full of this place. How could I leave it?

I knew that no matter how long I lived in New York,

part of me would always be a running-wild backwoods boy. When I was lonesome for Lostman's River, would I be able to close my eyes and see it? Would I be able to picture the creeks, the keys, the channels, the blue-green water, and all the creatures? Would it be possible to imagine myself back there again? I surely hoped so.

There have to be such places, I thought, places for birds and gators and panthers and, yes, even skeeters. I recalled Mr. Strawbridge saying that the governor's dredges would change the face of this land forever. I couldn't bear the thought.

If only the governor could see Lostman's River and all of the Ten Thousand Islands and the Everglades the way I did. Not as a place that needed changing, but a place that was perfect just the way it was. Not as a place for people to civilize, but a wild, uncivilized place. A place full of beauty that was not of man's making.

Maybe, I thought, I could help the governor see it just that way. If people like the Audubon folks enjoyed looking at pictures of birds and animals, maybe the governor would, too. And maybe if seeing the beauty of the creatures made the Audubons want to protect them, well, perhaps the governor would feel the same way.

I could draw pictures for him, I thought. Mr. Storter had said my drawings were good, good enough to sell in a store. I could send him carvings, too.

I will, I decided. I'll do it! I'll show him the river and the mangroves and the islands. I'll draw the deer and the panthers and the turkeys and turtles and frogs and tarpon and snook. I'll draw a rookery, with all the birds in their finest plumage, hundreds and hundreds of them! I'll show him the baby birds, their sweet, homely faces peering over the edges of their nests, their mouths open wide for food. I'll make him see it all.

Maybe, I thought, I could draw the picture that still haunted my sleep, the picture of the death-filled nesting ground. Yes, I thought, he should see that, too. Maybe he'd be more careful that the laws he passed were being obeyed. Maybe, too, in New York I could join up with those Audubon folks. I smiled. A crazy, bird-loving Yankee, that was me.

I could feel my fingers itching with eagerness to begin. I touched my knife where it hung by my side and, silently, I thanked Mr. Strawbridge for leaving me the beautiful pads of paper and lead pencils and paints.

Bean had said I'd figure out what I could do to help make up for what had happened to the rookery. And I had. I knew now how I was going to play my hand. It felt good, knowing.

Carrie came and stood beside me. I held her up so that she could see over the side. Pa and Mama joined us and we all stood together, looking out at the clear blue sky and the shimmering water that stretched out before us like a promise.

For the first time since we'd come to Florida, I felt hopeful that we could put the night of Samuel Davenport's murder behind us at last. And for the first time since I'd stood, horror-stricken, in the shot-out rookery,

I felt a stirring of hope for the birds and the gators and all the creatures who had shared the backwaters with us.

A pair of egrets flew over our heads, their white plumes flashing in the sun, their mouths full of minnows they were carrying to feed to their young. We watched them until they were out of sight.

Author's Note

The story that Bean Thompson tells Mr. Strawbridge at the MacCauleys' supper table is true: Guy Bradley, first game warden hired by the Audubon Society to protect the rookeries, was murdered just the way Bean describes. Bradley's death helped to raise awareness about the Audubon Society and the plight of the plume birds. As a result, more state and federal laws were passed to aid in their protection, and the laws were enforced more diligently.

However, the well-being of the birds and other creatures that inhabit the Everglades ecosystem was not assured simply by saving them from the hunters' guns. The process of habitat destruction begun by Governor Napoleon Bonaparte Broward's dredges in 1905 continued for many years, and is only now beginning to be reversed.

The Everglades and the backwaters of the Ten Thousand Islands depend on a continuous flow of fresh water that begins in central Florida near Orlando. But this flow of water has been disturbed, and the fragile, complex ecosystem of the Everglades is suffering, along with the creatures that live and breed there. As more and more people move to Florida, they demand an ever-increasing amount of fresh water. Moreover, big farming operations divert the water for irrigation and return it to the system filled with toxic pesticides and fertilizers, which choke the Everglades. Water management districts, not Mother Nature, control the water levels according to the needs of humans. As a result, the nesting grounds of many species of wildlife are flooded or left too dry, and populations continue to decline.

Efforts of individuals like Tyler MacCauley and organizations such as the Audubon Society, which helped to establish Everglades National Park in 1947, *can* make a difference. Many conservation groups and some Florida legislators are working to restore the Everglades ecosystem to health. Now, as in 1906, the future of the Everglades is in the hands of just one species: human beings.